# FORSAKEN TRUST

## Diane Wild

# FORSAKEN TRUST

# Diane Wild

 SUMMER BAY PRESS

# FORSAKEN TRUST

Copyright 2010 by Diane Wild

Published by Summer Bay Press

Cover Design by Wendy Dewar Hughes.

ISBN: 978-0-9868775-2-0
Digital ISBN: 978-1-927626-67-2

Louise and Suzanne
and my beautiful granddaughters,
Damla, Alara and Zara

My hope is that this story will give you a little
insight into your own history.
Although fictionalized, this story is loosely based
on the experiences of your grandmother's life.

This book is also dedicated to my mother, Ellen Clarke.
I pray that she has found peace at last.

# ACKNOWLEDGEMENTS

The idea for this book has been with me for a long time and I started writing it a few years ago. As I wrote, the characters became like a second family to me, always urging me on and wanting to have their say.

Without the help of my book writing coach and editor, Wendy Dewar Hughes, this story would still be only a collection of notes in a box. Her gentle corrections, enhancements, and encouragement transformed my ramblings into an orderly account of the lives of two amazing women.

Wendy, I thank you for that. We made a good team and I have found a new friend.

Special thanks to my husband, Barry for putting up with the many hours I spent at the computer while doing my research.

I thank my dear friends, Katie, Vickie, and Carole for your constant and generous support and also my nephew, Ian and my niece, Caroline.

# Chapter One

## Mary Clarke, Birmingham, 1902

Mary pulled the simple, muslin curtain back from the window and looked down the long, narrow street at the row of identical houses. At one time, she thought, they must have been well cared-for but now shabby doors sagged on rusted hinges, paint peeled and cardboard filled the gaping holes in broken windows.

She placed her hand on her large belly and felt the baby kick. It would not be long now. Her dreams of becoming a mother would soon come true. She brushed a limp strand of hair away from her face, felt the trickle of sweat between her breasts and plucked at the cotton dress sticking to her body.

Tommy would be home from the factory soon. Letting the curtain drop, she turned back into the tiny room. How cozy and welcoming it felt compared with the street outside. Tommy had lime-

1

washed the walls so they were white and fresh-looking and the hooked rug Mary had made out of old fabrics brightened the floor. Two stuffed chairs that had seen better days sat at each side of a fireplace, and with the few ornaments they had found, she and Tommy had made it a home.

This summer had been unusually hot. *If only a breeze would blow through*, she thought, as she made her way to one of the chairs and eased herself down, fanning her flushed face with one hand.

Tommy was fortunate to have the job at the factory. Other men were not so lucky. Mary knew that each day the men of the village crowded around the factory gates hoping to be among the few chosen for a day's work. Most of these men then took what little money they made and promptly drank it and most of their wives had given up trying to keep them out of the pub down on the corner. The children, gaunt and sallow, went to bed most nights cold and hungry.

Mary's childhood had been no different. Her mother, Clare, had given birth to nine children but poverty and malnutrition had claimed the lives of three of those babies shortly after birth. As the eldest, Mary had helped out with the last birth, watching her mother's agony as the labour gripped her. Trying not to scream, and too weak and tired to push, her mother lay on a filthy mattress with a single, ragged sheet and coats for blankets. The squalid surroundings embarrassed Mary in front of the midwife but there was nothing she could do.

Sally did her best to help with the birth, muttering all the while about the useless husband, though useless husbands were not new to her. She had delivered many babies in this poor neighborhood and so many of them had not survived. As long as she was paid though, that's what mattered most to her but she had felt sorry for Clare. She was different from the rest. Sally saw bruises on Clare's thin body. As Mary watched, Sally rolled up her sleeves and, speaking softly, encouraged Clare to push harder.

The tiny scrap of an infant slipped from Clare's body without taking a breath. Mary had held onto her mother, wiping her tear-stained face with her hands and begging her not to cry as Sally tore off some sheet and wrapped up the dead child. It was over.

Now, sitting in her own home, Mary remembered the pain her father's callused hands inflicted, leaving many bruises on the children's bodies. The screams of the younger children echoed in her mind as did the deafening crack of furniture splintering into pieces. Her mother often tried to protect the children by throwing herself in front of him so he would direct his rages at her instead. Only after he collapsed in a reeking heap on the floor did the terrified children crawl out from their hiding places where they had clung together crying and praying for the violence to stop.

All six children had slept in one room; three boys at one end of the bed, three girls at the other. Black mold climbed up the walls and the filthy bedding swarmed with fleas. Night after night the children woke crying, their bodies covered with welts and bloody from scratching but their mother could not come to comfort them. Mary lay awake covering her ears, trying not to hear her mother's pleading to be left alone. It always ended the same way, with the bed in the other room thumping against the wall and him grunting, satisfying his own selfish needs.

The few precious ornaments her mother had brought into the marriage had long since gone to the pawnshop, never to be redeemed. With only two hard chairs in the house, the children sat on the bare floor most of the time, or wooden boxes, if they were lucky enough to find any. On the rare days when her mother managed to afford food, she stood at the wobbly table and prepared vegetables for a thin soup with a greasy scrap of meat or a bone in it. The children scoured the markets for the spoilt vegetables that had fallen to the ground, rushing home with a precious bruised parsnip, a soft carrot or two, or maybe a rotting onion. Moldy potatoes would soon be peeled and thrown into the pot, the smell from soup making their mouths water. For a short time they would feel happy and full, but they were hungry most of the time. Even the beatings from her father were not as bad as the unrelenting hunger pains. Mary vowed that her life with Tommy would never be like that.

She sighed as these visions drifted through her mind. Thoughts of her school life flooded back, too, and she remembered how her tangled hair hung limp around her shoulders; her tattered clothes were torn and soiled. Most of the time her mother was simply too worn down to take care of these needs.

The other children at school would wait for her then circle around, poking her with sticks and pulling her hair. There was no escape. One girl, the doctor's daughter, named Joanne, was especially cruel, hitting her and shouting, "Dirty Mary, dirty Mary, and you stink. You have nits. My mom told me not to play with you."

Everyday Mary ran home knowing that the next day would be the same or maybe even worse. She tried to imagine that having nicer clothes would make the other children like her. If she had, maybe they would leave her alone, but she never got anything new, and they never stopped tormenting her. As the years went by she learned to suffer in silence. Besides her younger siblings, she had no friends.

When the lonely school years were over Mary found a job in a factory making bicycles. The dingy brick building was not large compared with other factories in the area. It had a broad wooden door on one side and a bank of windows along the front. Inside the cavernous workshop, five rows of tables had been set up where about twenty women stood assembling bicycle wheels. Mary's thin cardigan and dress gave her no protection against the unheated interior and the wind blew in the door and around her legs, making them numb with cold.

How vividly Mary remembered her first day. She had been instructed to work beside an older woman named Ida, who would show her how to do her job. Ida was a fat lady and had an enormous bosom that shook like jelly when she laughed. She was missing a few teeth and whiskers sprouted from her chin but she was kind and Mary liked her instantly.

When she had started, Mary watched how the other women worked so fast and worried that she would never manage to keep up. She was continually afraid of losing her job; the job that had taken her so long to find. When she shared her fears with her new friend, Ida just chuckled and gave Mary a friendly thump on the back that nearly knocked Mary off her feet. Mary stumbled, which made Ida roar with laughter and her immense bosom heave until the other factory women cackled, too.

8

# Chapter Two

When Mary had walked into the workshop, the other women had seen a beautiful young girl with long, flowing, auburn hair and emerald green eyes. Mary had never owned a mirror. Such a luxury would not have survived her father's rages. With no money to spend on herself anyway she had no idea how she really looked and had never thought of herself as pretty.

Tommy Clarke noticed how pretty Mary was the first minute he saw her but because he worked with a group of women who made him blush with their brash humor and raunchy jokes, he was careful not to show his growing interest. He knew both he and Mary would be butt of all their teasing if they should notice his attraction to her.

Tommy had begun working in the factory as a young lad and with his hard work and caring nature he soon became popular with the owner and the other workers. By the time he was twenty one he had been promoted to the position of department manager. He had been living with his parents and, unlike Mary's childhood, his had been happy and peaceful. Tommy's father, Henry, worked in a general store but these days the arthritis in his hands and back made every day a struggle. He walked with a stoop yet rarely complained. His hair had gone thin now and deep wrinkles lined his kind face. Tommy's mother, Gladys, fragile, stylish, and domineering, loved nothing more than having friends over so she could show off her latest purchases. She never noticed that her friends saw her as a bit of a snob. Henry simply doted on her and gave in to all her demands.

Tommy was their only child. While they had always hoped for more children they were in their late thirties when he was born, and after a difficult pregnancy and birth, Gladys was no longer strong enough to have more babies. Tommy had been much loved but never spoilt; they were proud of him. With his blonde hair and good looks and his success in school and his work, Gladys had high hopes for him to find a suitable wife and a prosperous career. She had no idea that he had already made his choice of a wife without his mother's involvement. He had chosen Mary.

At the factory, Tommy had a hard time trying to catch Mary alone. It seemed like she was always surrounded by the other workers. By the time she had been working at her job for a few months she had also begun to notice Tommy and blushed furiously every time he smiled at her. Between his attentions and the help and encouragement from her friends at work, she blossomed into a beautiful and confident young woman.

Things at home had not changed after Mary started working but somehow she found the strength to stand her ground against her father and had even prevented him from beating her mother a few times. She was amazed to discover that he was a weak, pathetic man who, once confronted, usually backed down.

Tommy looked for excuses to spend as much time in the factory as possible, hoping to catch Mary alone long enough to ask her if she would go out with him. She had been working there a several months already and he had still not found his opportunity.

Mary had learned to avoid men whenever possible but there was something about Tommy that made it impossible not to like him. He was always exceptionally kind to everyone, even the boy who swept the floors. He was so different from her father.

Sometimes she allowed herself to imagine what it would be like to go out with him but pushed that hope out of her mind. He would never be interested in her anyway, she thought, but on the other hand, it didn't hurt to dream a little.

One day at work Ida called Mary over to where she stood leaning on her workbench. "I need you to run a little errand for me, lovey," she said. "I'm too fat to climb all them stairs." She handed Mary a sheaf of orders and sent her up to the back office with it. Mary, thrilled at being given extra responsibility, smiled as she made her way between the tables and half-built bicycles to the back of the building. Skipping up the dark, narrow stairs she sang a little song to herself but stopped abruptly when she reached the top. Tommy had just pulled open the door of the office and nearly collided with her as he stepped onto the landing. He gasped, and as he stepped aside to let her pass their hands touched.

"Hello Mary," he said, ducking his head. Mary looked at him and nodded then quickly looked away.

He cleared his throat and stuck his hands in his pockets. "There is a new show on tonight at the theatre," he said. "I was wondering if you'd like go to with me."

Mary swallowed and gazed into his blue eyes. She nodded again. "Mm-hmm," she said. She noticed that her hands were trembling and dropped them to her sides, pressing them flat against her skirt.

"All right then," he said, with a crooked grin. "I'll call round at about seven o'clock. Where do you live?"

Mary's hand leapt to her throat. *He must not come near her home. Who knew what condition her father might be in?* And she couldn't let him see the hovel she lived in either or he would never want to see her again. Frightened but excited, she arranged to meet him near the theatre instead.

# Chapter Three

Tommy burst through the front door of his parents' home, face flushed and eyes shining. When she saw him, Gladys leapt to her feet as her knitting rolled to the floor. She was not accustomed to Tommy charging into the house. As usual she had a meal waiting for him and, as always, looked forward to hearing how his day had been. Henry sat in his favorite chair by the fire reading the newspaper and smoking his pipe. As Tommy rushed into the room, he put down his paper.

"Hello Mom," Tommy said, breathless. "I am going out tonight with a girl from work." He threw off his coat. "I have to get ready."

"What girl?"

"Her name is Mary and she lives near the market."

"Mary? I don't know anyone named Mary."

Gladys frowned. She knew about the kind of the

houses around the market; they were little more than shacks. Only the very poor lived there. She could not imagine anyone suitable for her Tommy coming from around there.

"Tommy wait," she called after him as he ran up the stairs. Five minutes later, he dashed down again and out the door leaving his agitated mother standing in the hallway with her mouth open.

Tommy could hardly wait to be alone with Mary at last. He stood on the sidewalk outside the theatre and watched the other people filing past the ticket wicket as he searched up and down the street for her face in the crowd.

As Mary rounded the corner, she saw Tommy standing there, his collar turned up around his ears and blowing into his hands. Late shoppers, loaded down with parcels, headed home against the bitter, cold wind. When Mary stepped in front of him, he smiled and reached for her hands.

"I'm glad you came," he said. "Let's go in."

If her mother had known about her plans, she might not have agreed to let Mary go out with Tommy. Mary had made the difficult decision not to tell her mother where she was going and with whom, just in case her father tried to interfere.

To Mary, the night was magical. She had never seen anything like this theatre and she loved its opulence and splendour. Velvet curtains slowly swung open on the stage and she held her breath as the show began. There were singers, dancers, and comedians. The air was filled with boos, hisses and cheers as the audience went wild with every act. Mary clapped until her hands were sore.

Tommy looked at Mary with her sparkling eyes and rosy cheeks. When she glanced back at him he leaned over and kissed her. He didn't know that this was her first kiss and that she could hardly breathe for the thrill of it.

Later, they walked along a path in the park together, holding hands and hardly feeling the cold. They talked and talked. Tommy told her about how he hoped one day to own a home of his own and have a family.

"What are your dreams, Mary?" he asked. They had reached a small lake in the park. How beautiful it all looked in the moonlight, especially compared to the street where she lived. She stopped walking and for a moment she said nothing.

When she answered her voice was barely above a whisper. "I want that, too," she told him, gazing into the dark waters of the lake. She felt sure it would never happen for her.

## Chapter Four

"This girl is completely unsuitable for you. Surely you can see that," Tommy's mother cried. It seemed to Tommy that she had thought of nothing else since he had started seeing Mary. "The girl's home is a hovel," she went on, "and the father is a drunken lout."

"It is of no importance to me where she comes from," Tommy replied. "I love her and intend to marry her." He could not believe that his mother had never even met Mary yet already she had dismissed her based on gossip alone.

"You can't mean that," Gladys said, stunned. "You hardly know her and I won't stand for it."

"I do mean it," he said tightly. "And if that's how you feel, I am moving out as soon as possible." He realized that could not live with his mother's interference any longer.

"Please, Tommy, don't do anything hasty. Oh, son, I'm sorry," she whined.

Tommy glared at her. "I'm sorry mother to have to move out like this but if you can't accept her, you give me no choice." He turned to leave.

"Oh, Tommy. Don't."

"Have you changed your mind?"

Gladys shook her head. "No, Tommy. I can't. She is not good enough for you."

Climbing the stairs slowly to his bedroom he closed the door, sat down on the edge of the bed and dropped his head into his hands. Silent sobs tore through him. He had never imagined that the happiest time in his life could cause so much sadness.

Henry tapped on the door. "Can I come in, son?" he asked. Not waiting for an answer he came into the room and sat down beside Tommy. Putting a hand on Tommy's shoulder he said, "Please reconsider, lad. There is no need to move out. She didn't mean it."

"Oh yes, she did. She meant everything she said about Mary," Tommy replied. They both knew that this was true. "She is asking me to choose between her and Mary and I have already made my decision. I love Mary, Dad, and I can't imagine my life without her." He sighed and his shoulders sagged. "But I love mom, too."

# Chapter Five

Mary was finding things difficult at home, too but in a much different way. Her mother began to ask her where she was going in the evenings and wanted to know who she was seeing. Mary always waited until her father had left for the pub before she went out and made sure she got back before he came reeling home. Though she knew he did not care for her welfare, she wanted to stay out of the way of his fists.

One night she sat by the fire at home with her mother after the younger ones had gone to bed. Her worthless father was out drinking as usual. She moved over and sat beside her mother, taking her mother's hand in her own.

"There is something I have to tell you, Mom," she said. Mary explained her relationship with Tommy and even told her mother that that they had talked about getting married. Clare wanted to know all about him and for the first time in years, they talked well into the night. For Mary, it was a relief to finally be able to speak of Tommy and she could see the love and support in her mother's eyes. They agreed that it would be wise to keep all knowledge of Tommy from her father as long as possible.

The weeks rolled slowly by becoming months as they counted the time until Mary turned sixteen. She and Tommy had been quietly making plans to marry but Mary knew that she needed permission from her parents. She also knew that getting her father's permission would difficult, if not impossible.

Now, with her birthday only a few weeks away, Mary decided that it was time to tell her father of her plans. Tommy had wanted to be with her when she broke the news. He wanted to do the right thing and ask for her hand in marriage, but Mary had refused. She felt that she had to do this alone and was afraid that having Tommy there could put him in danger. She knew that he had no idea how violent her father could be even though she had told him in detail about her childhood. Unlike Tommy, after all the years of beatings she was well-schooled in how to avoid the blows.

Waiting for the right moment was not easy but one evening when her father had a few drinks at home before heading off to the pub she finally saw her chance. As he sat by the fire with his mind clouded by alcohol, he listened to what she had to say. His quietness scared Mary. Suddenly, letting out a terrific roar, he lurched towards her, cursing as spittle spewed from his lips. "You'll not marry anyone, you whore," he screamed. "So that's what you have been doing behind our backs. Sneaking around, behaving like a trollop." He fumbled with his belt buckle, stumbling against the wall. "I'll beat the living daylights out of you."

For once Clare intervened. She rushed in and commanded him to leave Mary alone. "She loves this boy," Clare shouted. "If you hurt Mary he will surely come after you."

Albert staggered back and fell into the chair. Muttering and scowling, he pushed Clare aside. "I'll deal with you later, woman," he croaked.

Mary saw her chance to slip away while his attention was averted. She would give him time to mull it over and approach him again when things calmed down. Days passed and Mary carried on, hoping for another opportunity to obtain her father's permission to marry Tommy. Helping her mother as much as she could and even trying to be pleasant to her father, she couldn't understand why he had not mentioned the conversation since she had spoken to him. She lived in a constant state of nervous tension, expecting trouble to erupt at anytime, so it took her completely by surprise when he came home from the pub one night, not quite so drunk as usual, and agreed to let her marry Tommy. Mary was stunned. What had caused this change in him? Even her mother was baffled at his turnabout.

Some days later, Clare came home from the market with the answer. What they had not known was that the men in the pub had given him a tongue lashing when he told them his daughter wanted to marry some young buck. It seemed that they ganged up on him, shaming him by telling him he was lucky he had was such a good daughter who wanted to marry a fellow with money. But whatever caused the change in her father, Mary did not care. That night, she rushed to meet Tommy with the news that they could finally set a date for their wedding.

# Chapter Six

As he had promised, Tommy had moved away from his parents' home and was living in two rented rooms. Bitter and spiteful at her inability to control him, his mother had severed her relationship with him. Though he still managed to see his father occasionally, his mother would have nothing to do with either Tommy or Mary. Soon his relationship with his father also became strained.

With the wedding approaching, Tommy heard of a little house to rent not far from the factory where he and Mary both worked. Excited, they went to see it. The house was small, and as they went through the front door into the main room they saw that the walls were dark and dingy. In the back was a tiny kitchen with just enough room for a small table. Upstairs were two small bedrooms.

Tommy whispered, "Oh look, a nursery room," and grinned as Mary blushed. Every room needed paint but Mary thought the house was perfect.

They rushed to the landlord's office to secure it. Mary was thrilled by the thought that she and Tommy would soon have a place of their own.

The wedding was a small affair. With the help from her mother and the women from work, Mary managed to sew a dress from a piece of cream-coloured silk she had found at the market. She added delicate lace trim around the neckline and sleeves and tied up her auburn hair with a wide, cream ribbon.

Tommy watched her walk down the aisle of the church and his chest swelled inside his shirt. She looked so beautiful.

Mary's mother and her siblings sat in a row on one of the wooden pews. Her father had not come. Mary counted that as a blessing, knowing he would have arrived drunk and embarrassed them all. Tommy's father sat alone on the other side of the church. A few of the ladies from the factory sat in the pew behind him.

The week before, and without Tommy's knowledge, Mary had called on his mother, hoping she might be able to change the woman's mind about the marriage. Knocking timidly, she waited on the doorstep clutching her hands together to keep them from trembling. Gladys had opened the door with a smile until she realized who was standing there. Suddenly, her face contorted into an ugly mask of pure loathing. She screamed at Mary, calling her names and blaming her for all their trouble, and finally slamming the door in her face. Mary turned away in tears. She could not understand why this woman hated her so much. Her only crime had been to fall in love with her son. She never mentioned the visit to anyone.

Looking at each other now as they spoke their vows, faces filled with love and happiness, Tommy and Mary envisioned their new life together. Clare wiped her eyes with a handkerchief and prayed that Mary would always be this happy.

The small reception was held at a nearby pub. With help from her friends making sandwiches and salads and the pub owner providing the use of a small room off the back of the pub, Mary thought a palace could not have pleased her more. The barkeep's wife had decorated the small room with paper streamers hung from the old beams and a fire blazed in the gigantic stone hearth. For Mary, the day had been perfect. No upsets, no problems. She could not have asked for more.

Now a year had passed since their wedding day and their first child was about to be born. It had been the happiest year Mary had ever known in her whole life. After the wedding they had come home to this lovely little house. Tommy had carried her over the threshold and kicked the door shut behind them with his foot. Laughing, he set her on her feet.

"Perhaps I should make us some tea," she said, suddenly feeling shy.

Tommy took her in his arms and kissed her. "This is no time for tea, my love," he said. "Let's go bed. I need more than tea." He chased her up the stairs, and squealing and laughing, they fell on the bed together. Then the laughter stopped and he looked into her eyes while one finger traced the outline of her bottom lip.

"I love you, you know, Mrs. Clarke," he said. "You are my life and I'm going to take care of you always." Fumbling with the tiny buttons of her simple wedding dress, he slid it off her shoulders.

"I know," she replied, her skin tingling at his touch. "I love you, too, Mr. Clarke."

Then quickly removing the rest of their clothes, they slipped beneath the covers.

# Chapter Seven

Mary continued to work at the factory but it wasn't long, happily, before she was expecting her first baby. Soon, she grew so heavy with the pregnancy that she was no longer able to stand all day. That's when Tommy insisted she stay home.

He had been manager of the factory for some time and the owners considered him irreplaceable. He was a hard worker and his job was secure. He and Mary looked forward with excitement to the birth of their first child.

Mary's mother, Clare, had become a frequent visitor to the little house. Once her husband had gone to the pub she was able to slip out of her own house unnoticed. The two women chatted about things like what the neighbours were doing, the new baby coming soon, and how Mary's younger sister, Rosie, was behaving. Clare complained that, unlike Mary, Rosie would not help around the house or with the younger ones; she did not fear her father at all, and screamed at him if he raised his hands to beat her. Clare sat in Mary's kitchen wringing her hands, at a loss what to do about the girl. Having Mary nearby to confide in had changed Clare's sheltered life. Lately, she felt much stronger and had even started to visit her nearby neighbours - something she would never have dared before. Mary was pleased to see these changes for her mother's sake, hoping in time Clare might find some joy in her new friendships.

From Tommy's mother, they heard not a word. Even the baby's coming had not softened her stone-cold heart.

A dull ache now squatted at the base of her spine and Mary groaned as she pushed herself up out of the chair. She must stop this daydreaming and get on with making dinner, she thought, glancing at the clock on the fireplace.

The next day Mary woke with an overwhelming urge to clean the house. She remembered how her mother had frantically tried to prepare for the births of her children by scrubbing the kitchen table, then the floor and everything else in sight, even though it made little difference. Now Mary felt the same drive to get everything ready. That's how she knew the baby's arrival was near. By two o'clock the labor pains were coming strong and fast. Luckily Clare had called round and, taking one look at Mary's face, she rushed off to fetch the midwife.

With the help of the midwife, Sally, Clare managed to get Mary upstairs and had barely reached the bedroom when her water broke. Collapsing on the bed and gasping, Mary clutched her mother's hand. She felt so relieved to have her mother there with her. Sally was busy preparing the bed with special sheets, rolling Mary this way and that, oblivious to the groaning and panting. Sally had attended so many births that she knew Mary's labour was perfectly normal.

Smiling and making jokes, Sally patted Mary's arm. "Don't worry, love. Everything is looking good. In a few hours you will be cuddling your little one. You just see if I'm not right. I won't leave you until this baby arrives." This came as comforting news to Mary.

A few hours later Clare went downstairs to make them all some tea, putting plenty of sugar in Mary's to keep her strength up. It was going to be quite a while yet before the baby appeared. It was hard for Clare to grasp that her own child was now giving birth. Remembering her own birthing experiences, she now felt anxious for Mary and prayed for a quick, safe delivery. Back in the bedroom, she handed Mary the tea. Taking a few sips Mary fell back against the damp pillows, gritting her teeth through the pain of another contraction.

"How much longer?" Mary pleaded as pain gripped her, leaving her breathless. It felt like she was being ripped in two.

Suddenly, Sally shouted, "Push, push, it's almost here. I can see the head."

Mary gave one mighty push and felt the baby's body slip from hers.

"It's a girl, a bonny wee girl," Sally crowed.

Mary laughed as tears streamed down her cheeks and watched while Sally cleaned the baby and wrapped her is a small sheet then handed her to Mary.

Mary peeled back the sheet and looked into a little face frowning up at her. The baby's initial angry cries had calmed down to a snuffle. Tiny hands with perfect miniature nails grasped Mary's finger. Mary felt overwhelmed by such a surge of protective love for this tiny child that it almost took her breath away.

"Oh, my darling girl, this is a happy day," said Clare with tears in her own eyes.

Suddenly, Mary was startled when the bedroom door flew open and Tommy burst into the bedroom. "Are you alright?" he stammered. She saw the fear on his face.

Smiling, she held out her hand, motioning him to the bed. "Come see our lovely daughter," she said.

Tommy sat gingerly on the edge of the bed. Leaning forward, he kissed Mary and said, "I am sorry I was not here when you needed me."

Stroking his face, she said "Hush. Everything is fine. We have a fine, healthy, little girl." He reached for his newborn child and gathered her into his arms.

Clare gave Tommy a hug. "Have you a name for her?"

Together Tommy and Mary answered, "Ellen".

# Chapter Eight

Life seemed perfect, almost like a dream. Everyday Tommy and Mary discovered something new about their baby and basked in the wonder of their beautiful daughter. She was a quiet, contented baby. Though it seemed like she was always hungry, she seldom cried and when spoken to would gurgle and chuckle. Ellen quickly became a favourite amongst the neighbors and every time Mary took her out in the pram, she found it hard to get errands done because so many people stopped her, wanting to, "take a peep". Tommy was besotted with her and she squealed in delight when he came through the door; a real Daddy's girl.

Clare visited often but though Mary occasionally saw her father out on the street or going to the pub, she had no relationship with him at all and he was not welcome in her home.

One day Clare revealed that Rosie, Mary's

younger sister, had run away. No one knew where she had gone. Her mother had heard she was living with an older man and was distraught about it. "I know life has been hard with a father like yours, but I'm so worried she may end up in the same situation." she told Mary. "Your father roams the streets looking for her, screaming threats that he will sort her out once he finds her," she said, shaking her head. So far he hadn't found her and could not follow through on his intimidations. He was slowly losing his grip on the family as the children grew older and had begun protecting their mother from his attacks. Since Mary had left home, his brutality and viciousness had only grown worse. Mary wondered if he was also losing his grip on sanity.

When Ellen was two years old, Mary gave birth to another child, a delightful little boy they named Sam. He was very different from Ellen and always into some kind of mischief. Tommy loved to play with him, putting him up on his shoulders and bouncing around as Sammy squealed with delight. Mary knew this was how she had always pictured what a family should be like. Every day she felt thankful for her Tommy, and in her happiness, the memories of her own miserable childhood gradually faded. Her cruel father was no longer a threat to her.

In 1906, typhoid fever raged throughout the

country. The hospitals reported full to overflowing; everyone was filled with fear. In the poor areas the incidence of the disease ran rampant and vast numbers of people died every day. Mary helped her neighbors when their children came down with the fever and, knowing how contagious it was, she was careful to scrub her hands and change her clothes before entering her own house. She feared for the health of her own children.

One day Tommy came home from work feeling ill and Mary rushed to help him, struggling to get him up the stairs. He fell across the bed, too weak to move. She lifted his legs onto the bed, and feeling his brow, realized that he was soaking wet and burning up with fever. First, she ran downstairs and came back with water and a cloth to wipe him down, then she ran next door to ask a neighbor to fetch the doctor. Back in the bedroom, she talked to Tommy while wiping his brow, but he mumbled only incoherent words. Mary could hear the children crying downstairs so she went to them and while she held them close to comfort them the doctor arrived. He looked so tired, Mary thought, but nodding at her, he trudged up the stairs to see Tommy.

"I'm sorry, Mary," the doctor said, placing a hand on her shoulder when he came back down. "He has typhoid and it's pretty serious. You must keep the children away from him as much as possible. It is very contagious. It would be better for him if you could manage to nurse him at home," he added, "because the hospitals cannot manage as it is."

She nodded, choking back tears. "Thank you, Doctor," she said. "I want to take care of him here. My mother will help with the children." Already organizing in her mind how she would manage, she let the doctor out.

A short while later Clare arrived. When Mary told her about Tommy, she wasted no time rolling up her sleeves and putting the kettle on to make tea, her solution to all problems. After that she took care of the children, leaving Mary free to nurse Tommy.

Later on, after Ellen and Sammy were fed, washed, and tucked up for the night, she helped Mary bathe Tommy. It seemed to Mary that he had become much worse and was now delirious and sweating copiously.

"Oh, Mom," Mary cried. "What will I do if he doesn't make it?"

Clicking her tongue, Clare snapped, "You must not think like that. He's young and strong and he will fight this." But secretly she breathed a prayer, *Please God; don't let this sweet boy die.*"

For two days and two nights Mary sat by

Tommy's side, insisting her mother go home once the children were in bed, and watching him thrash about, his teeth chattering. He was so hot to the touch it seemed like the fever might burn him up. She held him in her arms, whispering her love for him. "Please, Tommy, fight as hard as you can. I need you so much," she sobbed helplessly before finally falling exhausted into the chair. Asleep, she dreamed of running through the woods calling Tommy's name, frantically searching around trees and scraping her legs on brambles. She could not find him. Suddenly, she woke with a start, her face wet with tears and her heart pounding wildly. She stared at Tommy. He lay still; too still. All of sudden, she realized why the house was so quiet. While she slept he had slipped away.

"Oh, God, no" she wailed. Reaching out, she gathered him into her arms. "Tommy, wake up, please wake up," she begged, praying for his eyes to open. Stroking his face and murmuring endearments, she kissed his cold lips.

Then, rising slowly, she walked from the room.

# Chapter Nine

Mary moved through the next few days in a fog of agony and grief, unable to grasp that Tommy was gone, wanting only to sleep, to forget the pain. Her only reason to carry on was hearing Ellen and Sammy crying for their Daddy. Clinging to her, they could not understand why everyone was so sad.

Sitting together in Mary's house one day after his death, Clare said, "You know I loved Tommy like a son. He was everything your father is not. But he would want you to be strong now, for him and for the children. I will help you as much as I can." She was worried for Mary and knew that she had not eaten or slept for days. The strain would soon be taking a toll on her health.

Mary knew her mother was right. The next day she announced with a sense of dread, "I must go round to Tommy's parents' house. There's been no word from them. They must be devastated."

Clare sniffed. "I suppose you're right, although I don't know what state his mother will be in. She most likely blames you. Perhaps I should come with you. We could ask Nelly, from next door, to watch the children."

"Thanks, Mom," Mary replied, "but I think I should go alone. She cannot hurt me now. I will go tomorrow." Clare was elated that at least Mary was making a decision.

The next day Mary set out. It was a miserable, grey day with mist rising and swirling around the gloomy street. *Just like I feel*, she thought. As she walked along the echoing street, a few neighbours called out to her, offering their sympathy and any help if needed. She felt humbled and cheered by their warm wishes and desperately hoped for a similar response from Tommy's mother.

All too soon, she once again stood before Tommy's parents' door, her heart pounding. She remembered her last visit like it had been yesterday and with hands trembling, she knocked and stood waiting for the door to open.

Mary barely recognized the woman who opened the door; she was so shocked at Gladys's appearance. Her once perfectly-styled hair now hung grey and stringy around her neck. She had always been slim but now looked simply bony. Deep creases lined her face but the same old hatred still burned bright in her eyes when she looked at Mary.

"How dare you come here after ruining my Tommy's life?" Gladys spat. "Because of you, we have lost our only son. He should never have married you. I told him no good would come of it, and I was right," she screamed, swinging at Mary with her fists.

Henry, hearing Gladys's enraged voice, came up behind, and restraining her, pleaded with Mary. "Please go. She is out of her mind over Tommy," he said, eyes wet. "I can't control her."

Mary stepped back, her hand to her throat. Tears streaming, she turned and ran blindly, bumping into walls as she slipped on the damp cobbles. She knew Gladys resented her but had not realized just how much. She hurried home to the safety of her mother and the love of her children vowing she would never again attempt a relationship with Gladys. If Gladys never knew her own grandchildren it would be her own doing. That thought made Mary feel very sad.

The sun was shining the day Tommy was laid to rest at the church where they had been married. It looked so pretty. Ivy covered the archway at the entrance to the graveyard and flowers bloomed over the wall, but all Mary could see was the deep hole in the ground waiting to swallow Tommy. Her knees nearly buckled as she laid the small posy of forget-me-nots on the coffin, sliding her hand along its smooth wood, and whispering goodbye. Clare stood by her side, holding onto the children's hands and weeping. The little ones did not understand what was happening.

Prayers were said at the graveside. As the coffin was lowered, Mary gently tossed the first clod of earth onto it and felt her heart shatter into a million pieces. People with whom she and Tommy had worked at the factory were there as were some of her neighbors. Mary felt overwhelmed to see that so many had come. Even Tommy's boss came, offering his condolences. Slipping an envelope into her hand, he whispered, "This is from me, and Tommy's friends. He will be truly missed. Please take it and let me know if I can ever be of any help." With that, he turned and was gone before she could thank him.

As Tommy's boss walked away, Mary noticed a man standing in the back of the crowd, hunched over, eyes red. With a start, she realized it was her own father. She glanced at her mother, back to her father then she nodded her head in his direction. He gazed at her for one long moment then turned and slouched away.

When it was all over, Mary reached for her children's hands but her knees could not hold her up. Tommy's father, Henry, stepped to her side and, wrapping and arm around her, slowly walked her away along the path where not so long ago Mary had walked toward her happy life with Tommy.

As they trudged back to Mary's house, Henry said, "I'm sorry about Gladys, lass. She is completely out of her mind. I have committed her to the sanatorium. You must never feel you are to blame for any of this. You made our Tommy very happy and I hope, in time, you will find it in your heart to forgive her."

Mary could only nod as she held Henry's arm. Pulling her shawl tighter she said, "Do you think you could help me get through the rest of this day? There's to be a small gathering at the house and I'm not sure if I can manage much longer."

Henry wrapped an arm around her shoulders and pulled her close. "I'll help you in any way I can, lass, in any way I can."

# Chapter Ten

After Tommy's death, Mary struggled to carry on as the weeks passed. Ellen and Sammy kept her busy. They did not cry so much for their daddy now but she could not seem to stop. "If only I could be more like them," she sighed, "even if just for a while." She felt so tired these days that even taking a nap with them in the middle of the day didn't seem to help.

One day about a month after Tommy's death, Clare came bustling in just as Mary finished breakfast. "I hope you have more tea in that pot," she said, dropping into a chair. "My mouth feels like cotton wool."

Mary leapt to her feet and rushed out the back door, holding her stomach.

"That's the second time that has happened," Clare said. "What's wrong?"

Realization hit them at the same moment.

"Oh no, not now!" Mary cried. "I can't be pregnant. It must be the upset over Tommy. It has to be."

Before long, Mary knew without a doubt that she was having another baby. She was sick almost every morning and her breasts were tender and swollen. She felt happy, then sad, then happy again. Knowing this new little life would never know its father almost broke her heart. She stroked her belly and vowed with more conviction than she felt, "I will have to make up for that. You will have all the love I can give, and we shall be all right."

It didn't take long until her small savings had almost gone, and without Tommy's money coming in things began to look desperate. The envelope given to her at the funeral contained only ten pounds, just enough to pay rent for a few more weeks. Mary was good at stretching a pound a long way but as careful as she was it would still not be enough.

Memories from her childhood scavenging for scraps at the market crept in and the old fears came flooding back. She must do something. But what? Her main concern was for Ellen and Sammy. She tried to think of a way to return to work, thinking that maybe with her mother's help she could manage, but with a baby coming who would hire her? The never-ending problems swirled about in her mind; never reaching a solution, never finding an answer.

One afternoon, Mary heard a tap on the front door. Expecting her mother, she had been busy scrubbing the table after rolling pastry, so wiping her hands with her apron and feeling a little annoyed at the interruption, she went to open it. To her surprise, Tommy's father, Henry stood there clutching his cap and shifting his weight from one foot to the other.

"Hello Mary, how are you?" he said. Without waiting for a reply he added, "I wonder if I could have a word."

Stepping aside, Mary replied, "Yes, of course. Please come in." Puzzled by the reason for his visit, she offered him a chair. "Would you care for some tea?" she asked.

Shaking his head, he said, "Not right now. I wanted to see how you are managing. It will be hard without our Tommy." Mary nodded as he went on. "The thing is," he said, "when he was a lad I paid into an insurance plan for when he was grown. Once Tommy took up with you, Gladys would not let him have any of it, but she can't interfere now and it's up to me. I want you to have it. It's not a lot of money but I am sure you could use some help right about now. I have set it up in the post office in your name so when you need to, please take it. I hope you will accept this in good will." He searched her face and when she smiled he breathed a sigh of relief .

"I am pleased to accept," she answered.

"I would love to see more of the children if that's all right with you," Henry said. "It was never my idea to stay away. It was Gladys who made it difficult." Shaking his head, he went on, "Where did all this hatred get her in the long run? It was eating away at her like a cancer. She'll never come out of that place, you know. What a waste of a life. Ruining her own life and poisoning all around her; that's what it did. The friends she thought she had gradually stopped coming round, and in the end she had no one but me."

Mary sat on the arm of the chair and, putting her arms around him, said, "Oh Henry, I am sorry things went so wrong. It was never my intention to split up your family. I only wish she could have liked me just a little. She has missed so much." They sat together like that for a few moments, both happy in the knowledge they could at last be friends.

Just then, Ellen and Sammy came running in from outside and stopped to stare at the strange man their mommy had her arms around.

"Come on you two," Mary said, jumping up."Say 'hello' to your Granddad. He has come to see you."

Ellen studied him for a moment then said, "You look a bit like my daddy only you're very old. Did you know him?"

Henry's bellowing laugh made them both jump then everyone laughed. Sammy was not sure what was so funny, but giggled just the same. Henry looked like he could not have been happier.

Later, as the children played, Mary told Henry that before he arrived she had been desperate to figure out how they would manage. "I'm having another baby," she said, her eyes shiny with unshed tears, "and this money is the answer to my prayers. I don't know how I can thank you."

Holding her hands, Henry replied, "There's no need for thanks. We are family now and I want you and the children to be happy." He put out a thumb and wiped a tear from Mary's cheek. "No more tears, young lady. You must not worry. Be happy about the new little one. I know Tommy would have been so pleased." He turned to go. "I will return soon, if I may. This is a new beginning for us."

Six months later Mary gave birth to a frail little girl and named her Sarah. The baby arrived too early and Mary prayed that she would survive. Clare and Sally helped with the delivery, both of them enchanted by such tiny perfection. Everything about her was miniature in size. Though premature, she was a fighter, suckling right away and clinging to life. She stroked her golden hair, smiling at her as she watched the baby pump her arms and legs with a determined look on her face.

"Can I hold her mommy?" Ellen cried, running into Mary's bedroom after Clare had cleaned them up.

"Me too, me too," Sammy chimed in, bouncing on the bed. Much to Clare's frustration, she could not keep them away.

Mary lay Sarah down on the shawl Clare had knitted. "You can hold her hand," she told them. "She is still too small for you to hold. In a few weeks you will be able to hold her." As they gazed at her, Ellen thought she looked just like a little cherub she had seen painted on the walls in the church. Sammy, however, soon grew bored and went off to find more interesting things to do.

# Chapter Eleven

Gradually, life for Mary settled down to a normal routine again. For the first few days Mary, still weak from the delivery, took every opportunity to rest and enjoy each moment with her new little girl. Sarah thrived and although very small, she stole everyone's heart. By the time Ellen was five and Sammy almost four, Sarah was walking and Henry's money was almost gone.

Fearing she might lose the house, Mary realized she must do something and decided to advertise for a lodger. It would be a squeeze to fit another person in because the house was so small but by rearranging Ellen's and Sammy's beds and putting them in the box room, which was not much bigger than a closet, they could manage. Sarah would sleep with her. She knew that she would also need to look for work.

Discussing the subject with her mother as they

sipped tea, Mary gently rocked Sarah on her lap. Clare agreed Mary needed some income. "I wish I could help you, love, but you know my situation. Your father has not worked in a long time. He is not drinking so much these days and has lost a lot of weight. I think something is wrong but he refuses to see a doctor. At least our Harry and Charlie are working now. Robert will be going into the mill later this year so just Sidney is still in school. There's been no word from our Rosie. I do worry about her," she said, trailing off.

Mary nodded. "If I find work, could you mind the children? I would even be able to pay you a little so it would help us both."

"Of course I will. Maybe you could get your old job at the bicycle factory back. Tommy's boss said at the funeral that if you ever needed anything, you only need to ask. It's worth a try."

The next day after breakfast and struggling to get the children dressed, Mary settled Sarah in the pram. Telling Ellen and Sam to hold onto the handles, they set off. Stopping at the corner shop, she asked if she could put a card in the window advertising for a lodger.

"Of course you can, love," said Jean, the shop owner. "It must be hard for you, trying to manage on your own. Let me know if we can help any time."

*How kind they all are*, Mary thought. She decided from there to take the children to the park. They had not had many opportunities to play since Tommy died and they needed to run in the fresh air. Today the sun shone brightly, the trees were in bloom and a pleasant breeze lifted her hair. It was a lovely day and she felt happy for the first time in a long while. At last she felt things were starting to go right.

Nearing the park, Ellen and Sammy began pulling on her skirt, urging her to hurry. Mary laughed. "You can go play now but stay in my sight," she instructed.

"We will, we will," they promised, dashing off.

Sitting on a bench, she watched them as they ran, tumbled down slopes, chased one other, and shrieked in delight with so much space and freedom. Mary rocked Sarah in the pram. The baby gurgled happily while reaching for a fly that buzzed around her face.

How Mary wished Tommy could be here to see the children grow. Sighing, she shook her head. *Stop this*, she told herself. *Think how lucky you are with three healthy children and a mother who will do anything for you. Be thankful.* When the sun began to sink toward the treetops she called the children to go home.

A week after posting the ad at the corner shop, Mary opened the door to a woman enquiring about the room. "My name is Mildred, *Mrs.* Mildred Cooke," said the lady, reaching to shake Mary's hand. Buxom and middle-aged, the woman's face was lined with deep creases so much so that her mouth turned down at the corners which made her look as fierce as she sounded. But her eyes were a lovely, deep blue and twinkled when she spoke. Mrs. Cooke hitched her arms up under her already ample bosom making it seem huge. In a coal-black coat with a felt hat squashed on her head, her appearance almost made Mary laugh out loud.

Instead, she smiled politely. "There is only the one room," Mary said, not feeling at all sure about Mildred Cooke. "I will take you to see it. You would be welcome to use the kitchen and living space, too." She was glad that the children were with her mother. Heaven only knew what Ellen might say to this lady. "My name is Mary and I am a widow with three children," she said. Mary saw Mildred's eyebrows lift ever so slightly.

"I have been looking for a place since my husband died," said Mildred. "His brother owned the house we were living in and now wants me out so he can sell it." At the bedroom door Mary stepped aside and Mildred sailed in, bosom bouncing.

Mary had purchased a bed for the room and hung new, bright yellow curtains on the window to match the new bed cover. A bunch of daffodils in a blue vase sat on the windowsill. Henry had been drafted to add a coat of whitewash to the walls and paint an old chest of drawers to match. Finally, Mary had made a blue rag rug and placed it at the foot of the bed.

Mildred looked around, nodding her head. "Well, Mary," she fairly bellowed, "I must say this is the nicest place I have seen so far. It will suit me fine. I will bring my things tomorrow if that fits with you. The sooner I get away from my brother-in-law's house, the better. I will give you a month's rent in advance."

Shaking hands on the deal, Mildred marched off down the stairs as Mary rushed after her. "You do understand that I have three small children and they can get noisy at times. I am hoping to find work, so my mother will be here in the daytime to take care of them."

Mildred placed her hand on Mary's arm and her face softened. "Don't worry, Mary. I love children. I only wish I could have had some of my own, but it wasn't to be. I'm sure we shall get along splendidly. I keep busy most of the day volunteering, so you see, I shall not be here either."

Then she yanked open the door and sailed out.

As Mary watched Mrs. Cooke march down the street, Clare came through the back door. "I tell you, our Mary, these two are going to get their backsides warmed pretty darned quick if they don't stop playing up. They have led me a merry dance this morning," Clare groaned.

"Come on, Mom," she said. "Sit down. I'll make you a nice cup of tea while I tell you all about Mrs. Cooke."

# Chapter Twelve

The next day, Mildred arrived with her few things and began making herself at home right away. Ellen and Sammy, shy at first, soon warmed up to her and chattered constantly as she sat in the chair by the fire, knitting fiercely. She did not interfere in any of the household schedules but was willing to help if asked. It almost seemed she had always been there, Mary so enjoyed her company and it was comforting to finally have someone to talk to in the evenings.

It wasn't long before Mary and Mildred established a routine around the house. Mary knew she must find a daytime job so, asking Clare to sit with the children, she set off to the bicycle factory. She hoped that Tommy's boss would remember his last words to her.

As she stood in front of the building a few old friends noticed her and rushed to greet her.

Hugging her and holding her hands, they chorused, "Mary, love, how are you? What are you doing here?"

"Hello, everyone," Mary said, smiling. "I'm hoping to get a job."

Nodding, they wrapped their arms around Mary's shoulders, and led her inside. Taking her directly to the office, her old working companion, Ida, knocked on the door then opened it, poking her head in. "Mr. Marshall," she said, "Mary's here. Would you see her now?" Then whispering in Mary's ear, "It's up to you now, love," she gave her a shove.

Mary stood in front of Mr. Marshall's desk clasping and unclasping her hands and fiddling with the front of her dress. She had not had time to rehearse what she would say. "Hello, Mr. Marshall," she stammered. "I came to ask if you had any openings. You see, I really need to work. Since Tommy passed, well, you know, it has been hard."

Mr. Marshall stood up and came round the desk. Grasping her hand, he said, "Of course we have a place for you, Mary. When can you start?" He noticed that her dress hung on her thin frame and she had dark circles under her eyes. He remembered the promise he made to her at Tommy's funeral when he had sworn to do what he could for this little family, if ever asked. It seemed he now had his chance to make good on his promise.

They agreed that she would come back to work the following week and Mary was soon home making plans with Clare for child minding.

Gathering Ellen and Sammy close on her first day of work, she explained to them that Granny Simmons would be taking care of them while she was away. As she held them, her heart ached to think of leaving them for so long each day, especially baby Sarah.

Ellen clung to her, begging her not to go away, and promising to be good. Mary explained to her that she had done nothing wrong and hugged her close to calm her fears. Sammy looked on, sucking his thumb.

Clare gave them a few minutes to say good-bye then suggested the children come and help her in the kitchen. They dashed after her, already arguing who would do what as Mary sat back on her heels, thankful her mother always knew what they needed. She felt relieved that she could take on this new role and not worry about them too much.

Life as a working mother was not easy. Mary spent long days at the factory before rushing home to relieve her mother and make dinner. The children, desperate for her attention, clung to her skirt, wanting to tell her what they had been doing and showing her drawings they had done for her.

Mildred usually returned home shortly after Mary and took up the task of helping to amuse the children and hold the baby while Mary cooked. After dinner she washed the children and got them ready for bed. Clearing the dishes with Mildred's help before finally collapsing in the chair by the fire, Mary ended her days exhausted. The weeks seemed endless.

Knowing Mary found the changes difficult, Mildred tried to encourage her. Patting her hand, she said, "Things will get easier once you get used to it, dear. At least you are able to manage now. Your bills are being paid, so take heart." Then she went back to attacking her knitting. The two women had become good friends and Mary was grateful that Mildred had come to her door. Though money was still tight after Mary paid her mother, she knew that without Mildred's help she could not have managed at all.

## Chapter Thirteen

Clare's days were full and the children were growing fast and so active that some days she could hardly keep up with them. Taking a few moments for herself, she flopped into the chair. "Give old Granny a rest now," she told Ellen. "Find something to play with." Sammy pulled on her skirt. "Play with me, Gran. Come on, get up."

Clare could take no more. She reached out and gave Sammy a hard slap across the face. Shocked, his chin wobbled and tears spilled from his eyes. She had never struck him before even though many times she had threatened to.

Clare, shocked by her short temper, gathered Sammy onto her lap, telling him she was sorry and gently stroking the red mark now clearly visible across his cheek.

*What's the matter with me*, she thought, offering Sammy a treat. *How could I lose my temper with the lad like that?* But she knew. Everything was getting to be too much for her. Albert's health had deteriorated rapidly. Coughing and spitting up blood, he was so weak that some mornings he could not get out of bed. She begged him to call the doctor but he stubbornly refused. He claimed he needed her. Even though the marriage had been miserable, now that he was dying she finally felt able to forgive him. It would not be long before he met his maker. Sighing, she got up from the chair. It was time to fix some food for the children again.

Sitting together in a few days later, Mary noticed how tired her mother looked. Though Mary didn't care about him, she could see how caring for both her father and for the children was draining her mother's strength.

"Mom," Mary said, "even though I know he's sick, it's hard for me to feel any pity for him. You seem to have forgotten how he beat you and the rest of us. It's because of him that Rosie ran away."

Clare nodded, holding Mary's hand. "I know, love, but he's different now. He can't hurt you. He's a pitiful sight. I wish you would see him and make your peace. He's going to die soon. There is no excuse for his past behavior and I will never forget about it. But he is my husband and your father. I will do what I can until his time comes and that's final."

As she lay in her bed that night, Mary's mind would not let her rest. Now that she was an adult and not looking through the eyes of a terrified child, she thought about her mother and the life she led. She gradually pieced together memories of her father leaving early to find a day's work then coming home angry and hostile, lashing out at anything or anyone. She realized how tired and frustrated she herself felt these days, bone-weary most of the time and with little patience for her children. She allowed herself to understand a little more of what her father must have been through. She could not excuse him, but could she ever be like her mother and find some peace in forgiving? She decided to visit her father.

Leaving Mildred with the children a few days later, Mary set off. It had been many years since she had set foot in her childhood home. Her mother, pleased she had come, hustled her in out of the cold. "Let me have your coat," she said, "and come in and warm yourself."

Glancing around the living room Mary could see it had improved only a little. With the help of Mary's younger brothers, Clare had scrubbed and whitewashed the walls until they gleamed. The place was still as run down as she remembered but the few changes that had been made were pleasing indeed. In place of the wobbly table they once used, Charlie had made a bigger, more solid table that was Clare's pride and joy. A fire burned cheerfully, giving off a warm glow that made shadows dance around the room. The biggest change in the house, though, was the calm, peaceful atmosphere. The tightness in Mary's chest gradually loosened enough so she could breathe again. Until then, she had not realized how walking through the door of this house had affected her.

"Your dad's in bed. He wants to see you," Clare said. "I'll come up in a little while if you want but I think you should go up and see him alone."

All the terror that Mary had felt as a little girl rushed back. She didn't want to climb those stairs and face him but she knew that she must. As she moved towards the bedroom she wanted nothing more than to turn around and run out of that house. Reaching the bedroom door, she tapped timidly then pushed it open.

*The man lying there can't be my father*, she thought. Once a big, strong, vital man, he now looked like just a wasted, shrunken shell. Looking at his skeletal face she felt like weeping. Rushing to his side and kneeling down, she took his scrawny hand in hers. "Oh, Dad," she cried. "I'm sorry I didn't come sooner."

Albert's weak voice croaked as he clutched her hand. "Mary, thank-you for coming. I don't deserve it. I've been a wicked man. When I think of how I treated you all it hurts more than the pain of this cancer eating away at me." Trying to sit up, he gasped for air before falling back onto the scant pillow but his eyes begged for forgiveness.

"I know, Dad," she said. "I know." Mary sat at his side until he finally fell into a peaceful sleep then she crept away, joining her mother downstairs by the fire. Neither of them spoke; no words were needed.

Christmas arrived in a few weeks and Albert passed away two days later. It had been a painful death. Most of the neighbors felt no sympathy for him, saying only that he had reaped what he sowed and he deserved what he got. But Clare and Mary, watching him suffer, could feel only pity. Surprisingly, Mary's brothers and sisters, though still bitter toward him, attended the small funeral, but only for their mother's sake. Rosie had been found and informed of Albert's death but would not come home for the funeral.

He was laid to rest on a cold, snowy day. The church looked as pretty as a Christmas card with snow blanketing the pathway and the trees, so heavily laden that their lower branches hung almost to the ground. A tiny robin sat on the fence and chirped merrily throughout the short service. No friends or neighbors attended to witness Albert's passing.

# Chapter Fourteen

Mary dragged herself home each evening after long days standing on her feet at the factory. No matter how many hours she worked, the money hardly stretched to buy enough food for the family. Her mother was also struggling to make ends meet since Mary's brother, Robert, had moved away to find work in another town. Though he promised to send money once he was settled and earning, nothing had come.

Since Albert's death Clare seemed to lose interest in the children, even to the point of snapping at them when they became noisy. It seemed like the desire to live had drained out of her. She didn't even want to sit with Mary or Mildred in the evenings, chatting and knitting, anymore.

Mary also noticed Ellen changing. Where once she had run to greet Mary when she came home from work, filled with chatter about her day, now she sat staring out the window, sullen and silent. Sammy always seemed to be in trouble while Ellen had withdrawn, staying out of Clare's way as much as possible. Only little Sarah, now toddling around, seemed happy.

Mary worried about the way her mother shouted at the children, and often smacked them for no apparent reason. Afraid to upset her mother, Mary said nothing and hoped the despair would not last.

Finally one day, she could not ignore it any longer. The changes she saw in Ellen made her nervous about Clare's ability to care for the children. "What's wrong, Mom?" she asked. "You are so irritable with the children that it's worrying me. They are getting scared of you. You don't want them to be like we were growing up do you, afraid all the time? Is there anything I can do?"

Clare face crumpled. Breaking down in tears and shaking her head, she said, "I'm finding it hard to cope since your father died. It should be easier now that I don't have him to take care of, but somehow it isn't. I don't know why. Don't worry, love. I will try harder. Everything will be all right." Wiping her eyes, she hugged Mary. "I feel a little better now I have had a good cry. I think we need a cup of tea. I'm going to see to that right now."

*If only*, Mary thought as she watched her mother put the kettle on the stove, *a nice cup of tea would solve her problems so easily.*

# Chapter Fifteen

A few days later at the factory, Mary was struggling with a piece of wire used in making bicycle wheels when she heard a loud snap. Looking down, she was surprised to see that her hand was covered in blood. *How odd*, she thought. *I feel no pain.* She heard Ida shouting for help and felt hands holding her arm up. Then blackness swallowed her. Sometime later, head spinning, she saw people standing around talking loudly, telling her she was going to the hospital.

"No. I must go home." she cried, flailing her arms and trying to get up. Before she could sit up the blessed blackness engulfed her again.

Waking up in a large ward with rows of beds running along each side of the room, she knew she was in hospital. As the room came into focus, she raised her hand and saw that it was bandaged to the elbow. Gasping, she pushed herself up with her other arm and looked around for someone to tell her what had happened. A doctor came into the ward speaking to a nurse as he walked towards her. With a mop of frizzy red hair and a beard to match, he looked like a bear in a rumpled, white coat.

"Hello, Mrs. Clarke," he said in a surprisingly soft voice. "You gave us quite a scare. My name is Doctor Brown." Smiling, he lifted her wrist to check her pulse.

"What happened?" Mary asked, sinking onto the pillow. "I only remember a loud noise".

"Well, as much as we know, your hand has been damaged quite badly by wire you were working with. We have had to do surgery. Hopefully, there is no nerve damage but we will not be sure until you have healed a little." Patting Mary's shoulder, he shuffled back down the ward and out of sight.

She had so many questions but the doctor had not given her a chance to ask them. Just then her mother bustled in. Reaching the bed and hugging her she cried, "Thank goodness you have woken. We were so worried. How do you feel?"

"I have to get out of here," Mary said, struggling to sit up.

"Now, don't you worry about the children or about the house. Mildred and I will take care of things until you get home."

"What will I do if I can't work?" she wailed, tears seeping from the corners of her eyes. "How will we manage? I'm only just scraping by as it is."

Clare took her by the shoulders. "Stop that, do you hear! You were very lucky. You almost lost your hand. I won't listen to such talk. We will manage somehow."

Clare explained what had happened and how she got to the hospital. Her friends from the factory wanted to see her. "They are so kind and thoughtful," Clare said. "They think such a lot of you and have already taken up a collection to help you out until you can get back to work."

Clare chattered about the children and how they missed her. She had news of Rosie, too. Since Albert's death Rosie had been visiting her mother. She lived in a rented, five-storey, terrace house. The lodging had been built back in the days of wealthy people and their servants, now long since gone. These once-beautiful homes had declined into boarding houses and brothels. Rosie lived with a man much older than she and Clare did not think the life she was living was any better than that from which she had run away. She had three children but seemed to have no time for them. Rosie had even told her mother that she wished she had never had them. "She's a very hard girl, now," Clare said, shaking her head.

## Chapter Sixteen

When Mary had been in hospital four days, Doctor Brown appeared and announced that it was time to remove the bandages. Gently, he unwound the gauze.

The gash wrapped around her wrist and across the back of her hand to her fingers. Doctor Brown examined it carefully making satisfied noises and nodding. "It looks really good," he said, smiling at her. "It's healing nicely. Now Mary I want you to try to move each finger one at a time, just a little".

Mary concentrated on moving first the thumb then the index finger but try as she might the next two would not move. She had no feeling in them at all. Of the last three, only the smallest finger moved at all.

Doctor Brown could see the panic in her eyes. "Don't worry," he soothed. "With exercise, you may get movement but I did warn you that there could be some nerve damage. Give it a little time. We shall see how it goes." He patted her arm. "Early days yet," he said, walking away, scratching his head and muttering to himself.

After he left, Mary tried again to move her fingers but nothing happened. Even trying to bend them with her other hand didn't help as they remained stiff and unyielding. Laying her head back on the pillow she gave way to a rush of tears. *How would they possibly manage if she was not able to work?* The income from Mildred was not enough to cover the whole amount of the rent which was already in arrears.

When she returned home the next day Mary was met with yet another blow. Mildred was waiting for her at the door. "Oh, Mary, I'm so glad that you are home again and just in time, too. I have bad news. My sister in Cornwall has had a stroke and I must go and take care of her." She picked up her handbag and threw the straps over her shoulder. "I waited for you to get home but I must leave right away. I hope you understand. I don't want to move out but I have no choice."

Mary could see Mildred's bags packed and sitting ready by the door. "Family comes first always," she said, sighing and wrapping her arms around Mildred. "Of course, you must go. I will miss you terribly. You have been a good friend." She kissed

Mildred's cheek as she pulled away.

Mildred dabbed her eyes with a handkerchief and squeezed Mary's good hand. Just then someone rapped on the door and Mary pulled it open. A young man stood on the street, smiling and tipping his cap.

"I've come for the bags, miss, and the cart's waitin' to take you to the station." With a nod, he reached for Mildred's cases.

Mary buried her tear-stained face in Mildred's shoulder once again. "Please write and tell me when you've arrived," she begged. Mildred promised to come back and visit when she could then turned and sailed out to door. Mary watched as the cart rolled away and wondered if she would ever see her friend again.

As Mildred disappeared from sight, Mary spotted Clare down the street with the children. Sammy tugged at Clare's skirt and pulled on the side of the pram. When Ellen caught sight of Mary in the doorway, she raced to her and flung her thin arms around Mary's legs as though she would never let her go. Sammy seized her other leg and begged her to tell him that she had seen lots of blood in the hospital.

Mary took Sarah from her mother's arms as they went inside and closed the door. Later, with the

Ellen and Sammy playing and Sarah asleep, Mary and Clare sat by the fire. Without two good hands, Mary knew that she could not work at the factory anymore and now she had no one to help her pay the rent. Mary felt sure she would never find another boarder like Mildred.

"What shall I do, Mom? I tried to think of something while I was at the hospital but no matter what I do can't see a solution. The money the girls collected from work will only last a short while. I am grateful for it but I must find a way to earn a living."

"You are having your share of bad breaks, dear," her mother said, "and I hate to be the one to add to your grief."

Mary gasped. "What, Mom? What has happened now?"

"While you were in hospital Henry died. It was his heart, dear. His neighbour came by to let you know."

Mary burst into tears. "Oh, my," she cried, wringing her hands. "That's terrible. How very sad."

Clare reached across the table and patted her daughter's hand.

"Things are worse than I imagined," Mary sobbed. "Any money he had would no doubt go towards Gladys' care, wouldn't it? Whatever shall I do?"

"I just wish I could help more," Clare said. "I will do what I can for the children but I'm afraid I cannot spare much else. Times are hard for everyone." The two women stared into the fire, each lost in desperate thoughts of insurmountable problems.

That night Mary dreamt she stood on the steps of the workhouse, her children crying, hungry, and scared. Waking suddenly with her body wringing wet and her hair damp against her face, she prayed for guidance. The next morning, after finally drifting into a troubled sleep, she awakened to someone banging on the door downstairs. "What now?" she moaned. Throwing on a shawl, she rushed down the stairs, heart pounding. She pulled open the door to find the rent collector leaning against the door frame, picking his teeth with a thumbnail.

Mary's stomach lurched and she pulled her shawl tight against her throat. John Roberts had the beady black eyes of a weasel and they shifted down her body and back up again. His long thin nose had a perpetual drip hanging from the end and greasy strings of hair sticking out from under his cap clung to his pasty skin. The long black coat that he was never seen without had earned him the name of "Vulture" throughout his turf.

"Mrs. Clarke," he sneered, leaning so close that she could smell his fetid breath. "I'm here for the rent. Ye're in arrears." He spoke in a loud voice to make sure the whole street would know about her situation.

"Please, Mr. Roberts," she begged. "I will have some money for you next week. Just give me a little more time. I have three children and nowhere to go."

"What do you think this is?" he shouted again. "We're not a charity! Pay me now or you have two days to get out."

"But," she cried, "I have no money to give you right now."

"You're lucky I'm allowing you that. If you're not out in two days I'll be sending someone round to throw your stuff in the street." Then he smirked. "Unless you would like to favour me with a little time between the sheets," he said, reaching to run a filthy finger along her neck. Mary slammed the door so fast that she almost cut off his arm.

It seemed like her worst fears were coming true. She would have to move from the house Tommy had been so proud to find. She collapsed into a chair, thinking about the dream she had the previous night and started to tremble. Then, forcing herself, she pushed herself to her feet again and took a deep breath. "We will never go to the workhouse" she shouted at the walls. "Whatever I have to do, I will do it."

Ellen wandered into the room, rubbing her eyes. "Who are you talking to, Mommy?"

"Go wash your face," Mary said, "then after breakfast we will go to Gran's house." As Ellen ran back upstairs, Mary went to wake up the other two children.

"That horrible John Roberts came round this morning," Mary told her mother later as they sat at Clare's kitchen table. "He's throwing me out the house. I'm behind with the rent. He said I have two days to pack."

"Oh, Mary," she said. "I was afraid this might happen and I can think of only one person who may be able to help."

"Who's that, Mom?"

Sitting back in the chair, Clare said, "Our Rosie. Her place is no palace from what I hear, but I think her front room is empty. She will want a few bob for it, mind. She doesn't do anything for nothing that one, even if you are her sister, but it's somewhere to go for now. What do you think? Shall I go round and ask her?"

"Oh Mom, would you? She may agree if you ask. I'm desperate."

"I'll go right now," Clare answered, reaching for her shawl.

As she hurried along the street to Rosie's house, Clare said a little prayer. "Please let her say yes." At Rosie's house she noticed the filthy windows and grimy door and groaned inwardly to think of Mary living in a place like this. Sighing, she tapped on the door.

After a while it opened and a scraggly, undernourished boy stared up at her. Wearing a tattered vest and dirty pants, his face was filthy, too. Clare swore she could see lice running in his hair. He confirmed it by scratching his head as he mumbled, "Wharra you want. Me mom ain't in."

But Clare knew better. "Rose, are you there?" she shouted. "It's only me."

Rose peeped round the door. "Oh, hello mom," she said. "What's up? You ain't never been here before so it must be important."

"Can I come in? I have something to ask you."

Rosie turned and led her down a dingy hallway with rubbish lying on the floor and filth smeared up the walls. What passed for a living room was at the back of the narrow house. A small boy and a tiny girl crawled on the dirty floor playing with a cardboard box. Clare cringed when Rose gave them both a sharp slap.

"Go on. Get out of here, you bloody nuisance," Rose yelled at them as they skittered away. Lighting a cigarette, Rosie flopped down in a chair that had stuffing hanging out of the arms. Gesturing towards a kitchen chair for Clare, she said "Well, Mother, what do you want to ask me?" She took a drag on her cigarette and tapped the ashes on the floor.

As briefly as she could, Clare quickly explained Mary's situation. "She needs a place to stay, Rosie. Could you let her have your front room for a while?"

"Well!" Rosie crowed. "Perfect little Mary and her brats have finally fell off the perch and now need something from me," she cackled. "I do have a front room that I was thinking of renting out but she'll have to pay. I have my own problems. My Len hasn't worked in a while. I could use some extra cash." Giving a sly grin, she added, "Shall we say three shillings a week?"

Clare looked across at Rose. *Where had the beautiful little girl she had loved and protected gone?* she wondered. Now her face was bloated, greasy hair hung around her head, and an unpleasant smell emanated from her unwashed body.

Clare despaired thinking of little Ellen living here. Sammy, she knew, would manage and might even enjoy having cousins to play with but what of delicate little Sarah? She only hoped Mary would be able to cope. As Clare's own mother would have said, beggars can't be choosers.

Standing up, she told Rosie that Mary would be round to see her and the room the next day. Anxious to get away, she pulled her shawl tighter around her shoulders to ward off fleas or lice, feeling like they were crawling over her already. She hurried out, taking deep breaths as she walked away down the street.

## Chapter Seventeen

When Clare got back to Mary's place she suggested that Mary go to the church and talk to the parish priest on her way to Rosie's place. "They have funds to help the needy," she explained. "Speak to a Father Sweeny. He's an understanding man."

Mary found him in the church and asked if she could speak to him. He invited her to sit with him on a pew. Turning to him, Mary told him of her circumstances and asked if there was any way that the church could help her.

"I have heard about your family from some of my parishioners," he said, taking Mary's hand. "Do not to lose faith, Mary. There are reasons why bad things happen and we do not always understand what they are but it will all become clear in time. I will pray for you." He promised to grant her five shillings a week until she found a job. Smiling he added, "As one door closes another one opens."

Mary thanked him and hurried away. It seemed to her that the doors just kept closing. At least with the allowance she would be able to pay for the room at Rosie's and still have a little bit to spare.

Clare had described to Mary the hovel where Rosie lived but to see it with her own eyes was still a shock. It broke her heart that Rosie's the children were so filthy and neglected. She could not understand how Rosie could treat her children so atrociously knowing how terrible her own life had been.

Rosie showed her the front room, hardly able to contain her delight at Mary's discomfort. The large room, bare and ugly, had only an old iron fireplace in the corner with small ovens on each side. *At least there's something to cook on*, Mary thought, relieved she would not have to share Rosie's kitchen. Old wallpaper hung in scraps off the walls; the bare floorboards were crusted and sticky with years of grime. Mary felt sick to think of her children in this awful place but she had no choice but to stay here.

Rose said, "It ain't much, I guess, but better than nothin'. Did mom tell you I want three shillings a week? I can't afford to let you stay for nothin'." She smirked. "Ye're not so high and mighty any more, eh?"

"Rosie," Mary began, "what are you talking about?"

Rosie cut her off. "You, marryin' that *manager*," she spat like it was a dirty word, "and actin' like the sun shines out o' yer rear end. You got what's comin' to you now."

With that she turned and sashayed out of the room. Mary could hear Rosie's chuckle as she sauntered down the short hallway swinging her ample hips. "She's no idea what she's in for if she manages to stick it out living here," Mary heard her mutter. She caught a glimpse of purple bruises on Rosie's neck and upper arms and she knew that Rosie was no better off than her mother had been. Her husband, Len, was the same kind of man as their father. He likely took pleasure in punching her senseless and probably came rolling home drunk every night. She had been so sure that Rosie would never stand for beatings like her mother had. She thought that Rose could always take care of herself. Mary realized that once more she found herself in a house filled with violence.

With only a day to pack up and move, Mary hurried home to gather what she could manage to carry. Nelly, Mary's next-door neighbour, volunteered her lads to help take the furniture on a cart the next day. Most of the women on the street were heartsick to see what had happened to Mary's family and tried to help as much as they were able.

Nelly hugged her good-bye. "You make sure you come back to visit," she said. "Don't be a stranger. We are all worried about you, and we will miss those lovely little babbies of yours."

The next day Mary left the children with Clare and headed back to Rosie's armed with buckets, soap and a stiff scrubbing brush. If she had to live there, at least her room would be clean. She stripped off the tatty wallpaper, scrubbed the walls then tackled the floors and scrubbed them until her hands were red and raw. Her damaged fingers made the job much harder but she persevered, slopping water and soap on the grime and watching the filth of years disappear. She was surprised to see fine, pale, oak floorboards under all the muck and, sitting back on her heels and looking around, she imagined how the house must have been in years gone by. Wiping the damp hair from her brow, she sighed, "I bet this was a grand old place in its time." Mary was a thorough housekeeper and suddenly, she had the idea that she might look for work as a cleaner at one of the big houses across the river where the rich people lived.

Cheered by this thought, she remembered Father Sweeney's words. "Ah" she thought, "this must be that door opening that he talked about." She started to hum in time with her scrub brush.

Rosie, passing by the door, couldn't believe her ears. She expected to find Mary in tears and would have loved nothing better, but she never expected to find her humming a tune. *Damn her*, she thought viciously, wishing now she had not taken her sister in.

Mary moved her furniture into Rosie's house, placing the two comfortable chairs each side of the fireplace, and her colorful rug on the floor. *Not bad*, she thought. The room looked quite cozy and by putting her bed on one side of the room and the children's beds on the other side she could just make it all fit. "Sarah will have to sleep with me," she announced to herself. "It will be a tight squeeze but we will manage."

## Chapter Eighteen

The children settled into their new home quickly. Ellen and Sammy loved playing with their cousins, Billy, the eldest, Louise, and young Freddy. Their cousins liked to get into trouble and had fun showing them exciting alleys and hiding places and new games to play out on the street. Mary's children did not like their Aunty Rose and Uncle Len at all and tried their best to stay out of their way.

Mary had thought that her life couldn't be any more miserable than it had been the last few weeks but she soon learned that living at Rosie's house was worse than she imagined. The screaming and fighting went on day and night, reminding her of her own childhood. Her children repeatedly scrambled under the bed clothes to hide from the turmoil, covering their ears and whimpering. Even Rosie's children, used to their mother's temper, found a safe haven with their Aunty Mary, often scampering to her room while pretending they were not afraid of the battle going on in the next room.

As the weeks went by, Mary stayed out of Rosie's way, too, going round to visit Clare as often as possible. One day, while chatting over a cup of tea, Mary said, "You should see the antics those little devils get up to." When she began describing them, her mother laughed until tears streamed down her face.

Mary had taken to including Rosie's children on bath night when she bathed her own three. They wriggled and complained like they had never seen water, and whined as Mary scrubbed them until their skin was pink. But once the bath was over and they were wrapped in towels on the rug by the fire, eating a bowl of bread soaked in hot milk and sprinkled with sugar, they didn't mind so much. She purchased a steel comb with fine teeth and some lotion to kill head lice and used it on her niece and nephews, and after lots of struggling, finally got their scalps clear and so they no longer scratched constantly.

Bath night exhausted Mary. After carrying several large pots filled with water from Rosie's kitchen, she boiled them on the top of the range. When there was enough water to half-fill the tin bathtub, she bathed five children and rinsed their shivering, wet bodies from another pot of warm water on the stovetop. Even though it tired her out, she was pleased to see her niece and nephews finally clean.

Rosie watched her sister without offering any help. "Why do you bother? The brats will be filthy again in five minutes," she sneered. But she wasn't about to complain because with Mary in the house she could go down the pub all day and night without the neighbors threatening to report her for neglecting her children.

## Chapter Nineteen

Mary soon found that the small allowance she received from the church was nowhere near enough to feed the children once the rent was paid. Clare sometimes slipped her a few coins if she could spare them but even with spending as carefully as she could her children always seemed hungry and always cried for more. She knew she had to find work and find it soon.

Leaving the children with her mother one day she set off to look for a job.

First she tried a few big homes across the river but the doors closed in her face. Walking along a tree-lined street, she could see more houses with lovely front gardens and sweeping driveways farther on. Approaching one of them, she went to the back entrance and knocked on the door. A young girl answered wearing a black dress and a little white apron and white cap.

"Excuse me," Mary said, "but I am looking for work. Could I speak to someone in charge?"

"You will have to speak to Mrs. Hardy," the girl told her. "She is the head cook and takes care of all the staff hiring. Please follow me." Leading Mary into a huge kitchen, Mary saw a large lady whose face glowed with sweat.

"Mrs. Hardy, this young lady is looking for work and I thought with Trudy just leaving you might need her."

Glancing at Mary, the cook asked, "What's your name?"

"I'm Mary Clarke, ma'am, and I am willing to do whatever work you can give me."

Mrs. Hardy looked her over. "I need a helper in the kitchen and a cleaner. Do you think you could manage that?"

Mary nodded. "I'm sure I could. When would you like me to start?"

"First you will have to see the lady of the house, Mrs. Simpson. She has final word on who we hire. I will get Betty, here, to take you upstairs for an interview. We will discuss when you start if she takes you on." She turned away and began pounding a batch of bread dough with both fists.

Betty signaled for Mary to follow her. "On my word," she said as she hurried along, "cook has been that miserable since Trudy left. I hope you get the job. We need her to calm down. Anyway, here we are." Tapping on a door, she waited until a voice invited them to enter.

Tiptoeing in, she said, "Excuse me, ma'am. There is a Mary Clarke outside to see you about a job." Betty stepped aside to let Mary to go in.

Mary took in the dark wood paneling, thick red carpets, and a large desk that dominated the room. An attractive older woman wearing a lilac dress sat behind the desk in a huge, velvet-covered chair. She had beautifully-styled blonde hair and the corners of her eyes crinkled when she smiled.

Mrs. Simpson stepped around the desk and pointed to two armchairs placed in a corner. "I do hate formality," she said. "Please sit down. I understand you are looking for work and it seems from the complaining coming from the kitchen, you have arrived in the nick of time." Her tinkling laugh put Mary at ease. "Tell me a little about yourself, my dear" she said.

Mary explained her situation as simply as she could while trying to impress on Mrs. Simpson how desperately she needed this job. Silently, she prayed she would be given the chance to work in this house.

"Well, my dear, I can see you are enthusiastic but do you think you could be here every day? You have three children. How will you manage?"

"I'll be fine, I assure you," Mary said. "My mother will be taking care of my children. It's all been arranged. Please, ma'am, give me a chance. I promise I will work very hard."

Mrs. Simpson sat back in the armchair. "I'll tell you what I will do, Mary. I will put you on a month's trial just to see how you manage and if you and cook get along you can stay. I do like a happy, efficient household. Mrs. Hardy is an excellent cook so we do not do anything to upset her," she said pointedly. "She will also show you your duties. I pay ten shillings a week to my living out staff. Your hours will be eight in the morning until six o'clock and if I'm entertaining I will need you for a few hours in the evening. You get a little extra in your pay for those hours, of course. If that's suitable, you can start tomorrow."

Mary jumped to her feet. "I'm hired? Oh, thank-you, ma'am. You'll not regret it. I'll be here tomorrow by eight."

She found Betty waiting outside the door. She had obviously been eavesdropping. "Come on, I'll show you the way back to the kitchen," Betty said. "You'll soon find your way around. Mrs. Simpson is a lovely lady to work for; very fair compared to some I've worked for in the past. Right pigs, they were." She giggled at Mary's startled face.

Back in the kitchen Mary informed Mrs. Hardy that she had been hired and would be starting the next day. "She is giving me a month's trial. I hope I can please her. She seems such a nice lady. I think I will like working here."

Cook gave a bellowing laugh. "She always says you're on trial then forgets and keeps you if you are working well. So don't worry; you'll do fine. The work is hard but I'll be glad to have you."

After her month's trial, Mary became regular household staff. Just as cook had predicted, her probation period was never mentioned again. Mary's main duties included brushing out the fireplaces and lighting the fires in the morning room and the dining room. She lit the one in Mrs. Simpson's bedroom first and also cleaned her mistress's chamber and scrubbed the bathrooms and toilets. The floors on the lower levels had to be scrubbed daily, too. She found that sometimes the kitchen floor was so heavily soiled that it took a long time to get clean.

As she went about her daily duties in the same room as Mrs. Simpson, Mary chatted away, gradually becoming comfortable in her employer's company. Occasionally, Mrs. Simpson invited Mary to sit and have a cup of tea with her once Mary's chores were done. Over time they became almost friends.

One morning, Mary confided, "I am so worried about Ellen and Sammy. It is such a struggle trying to make ends meet." The words came out in a rush. "I know you pay me well, ma'am, and I am so grateful for the extra food that I'm allowed to take home from the kitchen but with three children, all growing so fast, I just don't seem to be able to keep up. Ellen is awfully small for her age, and Sammy, too. Sarah has always been tiny but she doesn't seem to be growing. And now Ellen is having trouble with her eyes. I try so hard but it never seems to be enough."

After a few moments, Mrs. Simpson said, "Mary, have you ever heard of a charity home called Hope House? At a bridge party the other day, one of my friends mentioned the good work they do for families having difficult times. It seems you can place the children there until such a time as things improve and when they do, you can apply to bring them home again. I have an information sheet I can give you. It may be something you could consider." She went to her desk and pulled the pamphlet from a drawer.

She thanked her mistress, took the paper, folded it and put it in her apron pocket. *I could never consider doing such a thing*, she thought, going back to her chores.

Later, when she arrived at her mother's house to pick up the children, she mentioned the conversation she had had with her mistress. Showing her mother the information sheet, they sat together, reading and discussing it. There was a picture of the building in the pamphlet. It looked stately and grand and had beautiful grounds.

"You know, Mary," Clare said, "this place looks very nice and if you put the children in there it would only be for a short while, I'm sure. Maybe Ellen could get help for her eyes and Sammy could get better nourishment to build him up. You could keep Sarah home. She is a little young yet to be without you at night. I think you should consider it. It breaks my heart to see them looking so thin."

That evening, Mary sat by the fire thinking about what her mother said. The children had gone to bed hungry again. The only things she had to feed them were watered down potato soup and stale bread. All the money she had to last until the end of the week was already gone and it was only Wednesday. Without her mother's and Mrs. Simpson's help there would have been no food at all. Ten shillings a week did not stretch far enough. *What shall I do?* she agonized, pulling the information on the charity home from her bag and smoothing it out with her hands. She could not believe she was considering putting her own children there but could think of no other solution.

The next day at work, she went in search of Mrs. Simpson and found her in the morning room. "Excuse me, ma'am," she said, twisting her apron between her hands. "I wonder if I might speak to you about Hope House. I have been thinking it over and feel it may be best for the children for now. Do you think you could put me in touch with them?"

"Oh, Mary," Mrs. Simpson said gently. "I'm sure this is very hard for you." Putting her hand on Mary's shoulder, she said, "I will call on my friend to find out what you need to do. Don't worry. If it's not to your liking you do not have to put the children in. Just see what you think first."

Mary stared at the carpet at her feet and nodded then turned and walked out of the room, wiping her eyes with the hem of her apron.

That afternoon Mrs. Simpson called Mary to the dining room. "I have spoken with my friend, Martha," she informed her. "You are to go out to the home tomorrow; she has set up an appointment for you. I will give you a few hours off. The home is not too far away so you can get a good part of the way by carriage. Here are the directions."

Mary had not expected things to happen so fast but she realized that if she was going to do this then perhaps it was best to do it quickly. The rest of the day went by in a blur as she tried to picture life without Ellen and Sammy. By the end of her workday her eyes were rimmed in red.

When she stopped by her mother's house to pick up the children, Mary told her mother of her decision and asked her to keep the children if she was late getting home the next day.

Clare saw the anguish in Mary's face and wished there was something she could do, but there was nothing.

# Chapter Twenty

Travelling out to the edge of countryside by carriage, Mary rested her head on the window and reflected on how her life had changed since Tommy's death. Never would she have dreamt that she would do what she was now considering. What would Tommy have said? Shaking her head, she thought, *well, it doesn't matter now what he would have said because he's not here. It's up to me. I have no choice and I must do what's best.*

When she stepped down from the horse-drawn carriage, she realized she still had quite a long walk to get to the home. Thankfully, the sun was shining, she was on a country lane and the birds whistled in the trees as she walked along. A curious cow came over to the hedge and stared at her with her soft brown eyes, lazily chewing on a mouthful of grass.

*This has to be good for the children,* Mary thought. She felt encouraged as she walked along breathing the fresh, spring air. Rounding a bend, she stopped suddenly as she saw the magnificent home ahead of her. A large country mansion, it had a wide, gravel drive leading up to a formal entrance. Mary gasped at how splendid it seemed.

A wrought iron fence circled the estate and beautiful iron gates stood partially open before her. Mary slipped between them and walked up the driveway. She noticed a few low, long buildings to each side of the main house and she could see children busy doing chores.

Reaching the front door, she pulled on a bell rope. After a short while, a thin, small woman with mouse-brown hair opened the door. Mary explained that she had an appointment.

"Oh yes, you're expected. Please come in. I will tell Matron you are here." Bobbing in a curtsy, she scurried from the room and closed the door.

After a few minutes, a woman came in. She looked to be in her early fifties. Her hair was cut in a fashionable bob and she wore an emerald-green dress. She did not look at all how Mary expected a matron to look. The matron reached for Mary's hand. "I'm Mrs. Shaw," she said, offering Mary a seat as she sat down behind the desk. "I have been made aware of your circumstances, Mrs. Clarke, and want to express how sorry I am that you are having such a difficult time. You must not feel that coming to us is a last resort. On the contrary, we can help make a new start for you and your children. I don't know what you have been told about our work but let me reassure you, if you decide to leave your children with us and later you change your mind, you can reclaim them at any time. This home is funded by some very wealthy people whose only wish is to help people like you." Smiling, she reached across the desk and pressed Mary's hand.

Mrs. Shaw seemed so sensitive and caring that Mary felt at ease at once. "Thank-you, Mrs. Shaw," Mary said, "but I have some questions."

For the next half hour she found out all she believed she needed to know about the home. Feeling satisfied with Mrs. Shaw's explanations, she agreed she would admit Ellen first. She told the matron that Sammy was not well but as soon as he recovered he would come, too. Convinced that this was the best solution to care for her children, and now having seen the home, she felt comfortable with her decision.

Mrs. Shaw stood up, smoothing her dress. She pulled a sheaf of papers from a drawer for Mary to sign authorizing consent for the control of Ellen and Sammy while they were in the care of the home.

Mary hesitated, pen in hand.

"Do you have another question, Mary?" Mrs. Shaw enquired.

"It's hard," Mary said. "I feel like I'm signing away my children."

Mrs. Shaw patted her arm. "It's not like that at all," she said. "We're just here to help during your time of need."

Mary nodded and signed her name.

Leaving Hope House, Mary had a spring in her step that had not been there for a long time. Hurrying back to Clare's, she could hardly wait to tell her mother all about the lovely old buildings and vast grounds. She pictured her children playing outside and becoming strong and healthy again and felt relieved that she could bring them here. Mary strode down the lane completely unaware that a dark cloud hovered on the horizon that would change the course of her life forever.

# Chapter Twenty-one

Ellen, at seven years old, had changed from a bubbly, energetic child into a quiet, unhappy little girl. Living in Rosie's house made her anxious and jumpy, and she ran and hid whenever she saw her Uncle Len or Aunt Rose coming.

Once Mary had made the decision to move Ellen to Hope House she knew she had to prepare her for the change, but there was so little time. Mary had agreed to bring Ellen to the home two days hence. That evening she pulled Ellen onto her lap.

"There is something I have to tell you, Ellen," she said. "I know that you don't like living here with Aunty Rosie and Uncle Len so I have found another house where you can live. It is a big, beautiful house and there are lots of other children living there. There is plenty to eat, too, so you won't be hungry anymore."

"What house, Mommy?" Ellen gasped, clutching Mary's sleeves.

"It's a house in the country with a big garden. You can stay there for a while, just until I find us another place to live so we can move away from here. Would you like that, Ellen?"

Ellen's eyes filled with tears. "I don't want to go away," she whimpered. "I want to stay where you are."

"Of course you do, darling, and I want that, too, but this is just for a while until things get better for us. Once Sammy feels better, he can come, too."

"Will Sarah come?" Ellen asked.

"She's too little still," Mary said. "But don't worry. I think you will really like it at Hope House." Mary kissed the top of Ellen's head and pulled her close. "It will be fine," she said, swallowing. "You'll see." She hoped with all her heart that she was right.

Two days later, Mary stood on the steps of Hope House again and rang the bell. On the journey there Ellen had been excited about the cows she saw in the meadows and the woolly sheep munching grass on the hillsides. She skipped along beside Mary chattering, "Will I be able to ride on a cow? Do they have a horse? Will I get pudding?"

Mary was pleased that Ellen seemed so happy but now she could hardly bear to look into Ellen's eyes as her daughter looked up at her with a quivering smile. They waited for someone to answer the door and Mary felt like her heart would shatter. She wanted to remember the feel of Ellen's hand in hers, the smell of her soft skin and the colour of her eyes. Mary felt as though she was relinquishing her child into the abyss.

The beautiful, carved wooden door opened. The same small woman who had answered the door before, timidly invited them in and led them to the office.

"Matron will be with you in a moment," she said, scurrying from the room.

"Oh, my goodness, she's like a little scared rabbit," Mary said.

Ellen giggled.

Mrs. Shaw came bustling in. "Ah, Mrs. Clarke," she said. "How good it is to see you." Unsmiling, she pulled some papers from a pile on her desk. "This must be, let's see," she ran her finger down the page in front of her, "oh, yes, Ellen. Come over here, Ellen," she demanded. Mary let go of Ellen's hand and nodded for her to obey. Bending down, Mrs. Shaw grasped Ellen by the chin and inspected her face. "What a lovely little thing she is," she said, as though Ellen was an object one might pick up from a desktop. "Once we fatten her up a little she might be quite pretty."

Turning to Mary, she said, "Where is the boy? I thought you were to bring him today."

Mary reached out and drew Ellen back to her side. "He's still quite ill," she said quietly. "He is not able to travel yet."

"Well, we would like him here as soon as you can bring him. It does upset the bookkeeping when we have to explain to our sponsors that there is a shortfall."

"I understand," Mary said, "but Ellen is here now. If you're ready I can go with her to help her settle in."

"What?" Mrs. Shaw said, all neighbourly kindness gone. "Oh, no, that's completely out of the question, my dear. We find that children settle down best once you're gone. The sooner you leave the better. She will be perfectly fine. Don't worry. Just say your good-byes quickly and get it over with. She is bound to cry. Take no notice."

Mary was stunned at the woman's cold attitude. "Right now? But she's not ready," she said, hanging onto Ellen.

"Come, come, woman. Do not make it worse for the child." Grasping Ellen by her shoulders she commanded, "Say goodbye to your mother. She has to go back home now."

Suddenly Ellen realized that her mother was leaving her with this nasty woman. She screamed, "Mommy, don't leave me here. I want to go home now." Before she could run to her mother's side, Mrs. Shaw picked her up and marched through a door at the side of the room then closed the door. Mary heard it lock after her. She could hear Ellen's screams through the solid wood door and the sound of her little hands banging and scratching on its smooth surface. The last words that Mary heard from her sobbing daughter were, "I want my Mommy."

On the other side of that door, Mrs. Shaw picked Ellen up off the floor and slapped her on the side of the head. "Now, young lady, you are in our care. Your mother did not want you anymore so from now on you will do as we say." A thin cry escaped from Ellen's throat. "Stop your sniffling, now," Mrs. Shaw told her. "We'll find a place for you."

A young girl of about ten years old entered the room. "Ellen, go with Ruth here. She will show you where you are to sleep." Silently, Ruth motioned for Ellen to follow her then grabbed Ellen's hand and hurried from the room.

A few minutes later, Mrs. Shaw returned to the office, tugging at her blouse and patting her hair. She assured Mary that Ellen would soon settle once she made a few friends. "I'm sorry we had to do it that way, but we find it works better than dragging it out. I recommend that you do not try to visit Ellen for a while as this disrupts the breaking away process."

"But," Mary said, shocked, "you told me that I would be able to see Ellen whenever I like. How long is this process supposed to take?"

"We've found that it takes at least six months."

"Six months!" Mary cried. "Oh no, I couldn't leave her that long. She's only seven years old. Please make an exception," she begged.

"I'm afraid you have no choice, Mrs. Clarke. You signed those papers and now we have complete control of Ellen. You must respect our rules. Now, I will show you out. Please let me know when you will bring Sammy."

The door of Hope House closed behind her and Mary stood outside, staring unseeing at the ground in front of her. What had just happened? She knew that inside that building somewhere Ellen would be crying for her. Mary knew that Ellen needed her mommy to hold her and comfort her. *What have I done? I have lost my child.* Sobbing, she ran the length of the long drive. At the iron gates, she collapsed on the ground. Anguished cries escaped from her belly as she clung to the black, iron bars.

Only a few minutes before they had passed through those gates and she had held Ellen's hand as she had skipped happily into what they both thought was a better future.

After she cried herself dry, she stood up, brushed the leaves and soil from her clothes and started for home. She hardly remembered the journey back to her mother's house where she burst through the front door sobbing. Clare was banking the fire and turned, startled. "Whatever is the matter, Mary?" she cried, running to her.

"Oh Mom, they've taken Ellen. I thought it was such a nice place but the matron was horrid to me. I tried to bring Ellen back but they snatched her away. I'm not allowed to see her for a months and months."

"Oh, my Mary," Clare crooned, rocking Mary in her embrace. "How could this happen? I felt so sure that this would be the answer for you. What will become of our darling, little Ellen?"

Mary stood back and wiped her eyes with the back of her hand. "One thing I know for sure," she said, "Sammy will not be going to that place no matter what they said."

## Chapter Twenty-two

### Ellen Clarke, 1909

A long hallway ran the length of Hope House. The walls, painted dark brown, stretched ominously before her as Ellen followed the girl named Ruth down the hall. Ruth had two brown braids down her back that nearly touched her waist and she wore a brown uniform. They reached a long dormitory filled with cots lined up in neat rows against the walls and Ruth led her into the room.

"This will be your bed," Ruth said, leading Ellen to a cot. "We have to wear uniforms here and yours should be in that cupboard by the bed. Oh, do stop that crying," she snapped. "You'll only get teased by the older ones. They can be very nasty to the new children."

Ellen wiped her nose with her sleeve and obeyed. Then she noticed a bag on the bed. "That's my mommy's bag," she said, spinning around to find her mother.

"It will have a few of your things from home that she left for you," Ruth explained. "She's given you away, just like my mother did. Put it in the cupboard now and follow me to the dining room."

Ellen did as she was told and went with Ruth back down the dark hallway. They turned in at another door. "This is where we eat. You've missed lunch, so you have to wait now until dinner time before you get to eat."

Ellen gazed around the massive room. She had never seen anything like it. A beautiful ceiling, decorated with carved garlands and little angels loomed high above and tall windows looked out onto the gardens beyond. Rows of tables with benches lined the entire room. *There must be lots of children here*, she thought.

Ruth said, "I must go now as I have lots of chores to do. It's no picnic here. You'll have to find your way back to your dorm by yourself." Then she walked away leaving Ellen all alone.

Ellen tiptoed back down the long hallway with one hand on the wall. She tried not to make a sound. The room was still empty so she opened the cupboard and drew out the bag that her mother had left. Holding it tight against her chest, she smelled the scent of the soap her mother used and began to cry. Lying down on the bed, she closed her eyes. The rough woolen blanket scratched her face but Ellen hardly noticed over the pain in her chest. She wanted her mother. She lay there a long time, her face buried in the bag holding her few belongings from home.

After a while, Ellen felt a tap on her shoulder and looked up. Moving the bag aside she saw a girl about her own age standing next to her bed.

"Hello," the girl said. "I'm Margaret. Who are you?"

"I'm Ellen and I want to go home." Her bottom lip began to tremble again.

"Well, you won't be allowed. My mother left me here a long time ago. Stop crying," she told her. "No one cares here. It will soon be time to eat so let's go to the dining room now. We have to hurry or all the food will be gone."

Ellen stuffed her bag back in the cupboard and followed Margaret to the dining room. This time lots of children were seated at the long tables and their chatter filled the room. Margaret told Ellen to sit at the first table. "That way, if there's any food left over we can get seconds."

Ellen had not eaten since morning, and even then it had been only a slice of stale bread with margarine. There had been nothing else in the pantry at home.

When a plate of stew was placed in front of her,

Ellen's mouth watered. She never had food like this at home. Cheering up, she gobbled it down hoping there would be more, and much to her delight, there was. The stew was followed by hot suet pudding with custard.

Suddenly, the room went quiet. Ellen looked around to see what had happened and saw the horrible matron stride in, clapping her hands for order.

"Children," she shouted, "I want you to go to your rooms quietly in single file. You will all check the roster sheet for your duties tomorrow." A loud groan rose from the older children.

"Less of that or you will have double duty," matron bellowed then strode from the room.

Ellen leaned toward Margaret. "What's a roster?" she whispered.

"Come with me and I'll show you," she answered. "You'll soon learn." Grabbing Ellen's hand, she hurried off to another large hall. On the way, Ellen noticed the same office where she had arrived with her mother. Dashing to it she flung the door open, calling for her.

"What are you doing here?" matron shrieked. She sounded just like Ellen's Aunty Rose.

"I am looking for my mommy," Ellen cried. "I want to go home."

Matron handed a batch of papers to another lady

in a starched apron and marched across the room. Slapping Ellen hard on the face, she hissed, "Get out of here, you little brat." She pushed her out the door and slammed it closed behind her.

Margaret took Ellen's hand. "Never speak to matron like that again. She is mean and nasty and she likes to hit us. Let's hope she forgets about you or you will get another beating." Together, they ran back to the dormitory where Ellen flung herself beneath the blanket on her bed, pulling it up over her head and trembling.

She thought about the things her mother had told her before coming here. "Be a good girl, Ellen," she had said, "and do as you are told. I will come for you and Sammy as soon as I am able."

Now Ellen knew that this was not true. Her mother had lied to her, had given her away, but kept Sammy. *Why had this terrible thing happened?* The only answer she could find was that her mother no longer loved her. Ellen had no way of knowing that at that very moment her mother sat at home crying from a broken heart.

# Chapter Twenty-three

Ellen soon found out that her days were very different from what she was used to. Early every morning, a staff member marched down the dormitory shouting, "Get up, you lazy lot," and banging on the beds with a wooden bat. Those that were too slow were slapped. "Go for your breakfast and hurry," the women shouted. "You have lots of chores to do."

Scurrying to get dressed, Ellen and her new friend, Margaret, rushed to the dining room. Day after day, breakfast was the same, a bowl of porridge and a cup of hot, sweet tea. Whatever she was served, Ellen loved. She had been hungry most of the time at home so she was happy to have what seemed like so much food. When she heard some of the bigger girls grumble about it she could never understand why.

Ellen also soon got used to the routine at Hope House. Her main duties were in the kitchen where she stood on a small box scrubbing vegetables for the cook, Mrs. White. Later, an older girl showed her how to wash dishes. Except for mealtimes and bedtime, Ellen worked all day in the hot kitchen among the steaming pots. Sometimes Cook grew irritated with her if she was not fast enough, but she never struck her.

One day while walking back to their dorm, Margaret said, "You are lucky to be in the warm kitchen. All the other rooms are freezing cold, especially in winter."

Ellen constantly watched for her brother, Sammy. Her mother had said once he was feeling well he would be coming into the home but she had been here a long time and seen no sign of him. Because she had not seen anyone from her family since being admitted into the home, she had no way of knowing Sammy was sick with typhoid fever and had been admitted to the fever hospital. Ellen didn't know that after losing her the way she had Mary had no intention of sending Sammy to Hope House even after he recovered.

Ellen missed her family and every night she prayed that her mom or her gran would come and take her home. But spring turned to summer then summer became autumn and still no one came. Little by little Ellen gave up hope and little by little a seed of anger grew in her toward her mother.

One morning after breakfast, matron came bustling in to the dining room and called all of the children to the main hall. Once everyone had assembled, she clapped her hands for quiet.

"Now children, we have exciting news. In a few days you are all going on a long trip by sea. This is wonderful thing. You are going on a big adventure and will be adopted by families in other countries and get to live in lovely homes."

Some older children jumped up and down and cheered. "At last," they said, filled with excitement, "we are getting away from here."

Ellen did not understand what was happening. "What does adopt mean?" she asked Margaret. Her friend just shrugged her shoulders. She did not know what it meant either.

Over the next two days the staff bustled about organizing the children into groups. Ellen and Margaret were put in Group B and told they would go to Canada. Group A would go to Australia and Group C to South Africa. Few of the children understood what was going to happen only that they would be going on a train and a ship. They were excited about that since most had never travelled on a train before.

The next day the staff woke them up in the usual way, telling them, "Today is the day you leave Hope

House. After breakfast you must assemble at the front entrance. You will be taken to the train station so please take all your belongings from the cupboard by your bed as you will not be coming back."

## Chapter Twenty-four

The children stood on the platform at the station, the older girls happily chattering together while the younger ones' shoulders shuddered as they hiccupped and sobbed.

Ellen scanned the crowd hoping to see her mother, thinking surely she would come to see her off but she could not see her anywhere. Loudspeakers boomed messages and porters rushed by with luggage piled high on trolleys shouting, "Out of the way; coming through."

The train pulled in amidst a cloud of hissing and puffing, the steam from its stack engulfing the small, frightened children. The staff gathered them all into their groups, instructing them to get ready to board. Slowly they filed onto the train.

Luckily, Ellen was able to sit by the window next to Margaret. They held hands, eyes shining with excitement. "I wonder what it'll be like," Ellen said.

Margaret replied, "Well, they said we are going to nice homes and it has to be better than Hope House. Maybe we can live together in Canada."

"Where's Canada?" Ellen asked.

"I don't know," Margaret replied looking out the window as the train pulled away from the station.

At the docks in Liverpool, the groups of children were separated and prepared to board. Ellen stood in awe, gazing up at the huge ship. High up on the side near the front, in bold white letters, she saw a name painted but she couldn't read so did not know that the ship's name was the S.S. Scandinavian.

"Come along, children," Matron said. Once she had boarded them her job was done, and she looked forward to a nice little bonus. *Things are certainly going well,* she thought, anxious to get back to the home and prepare the new batch for immigration. For her, poverty was proving very profitable.

Ellen and Margaret were shown to the lower decks where lots of cots had been set up in one long space. Ellen, pleased to find out she would be with Margaret for the journey, was so excited to be on a ship that being crowded together did not matter.

By now, she and Margaret were hungry and thirsty. They had not eaten since breakfast and it was late in the afternoon before the ship got underway. As soon as they were told to make their way to the eating area, the children stampeded, scrambling for seats at the long tables, their mouths watering from the smell of food.

Each table had a number. "Go to the large table at the end of the room with your plates to be served, once your table number is called," bellowed the staff.

Chicken, mashed potatoes and peas were followed by rice pudding and hot sweet tea. *This food is even better than back at Hope House*, Ellen thought, as she gulped down the last of her tea. With their bellies full, they made their way back to their beds. By now most of the children collapsed on the cots, exhausted from their long day.

The next morning they woke to a different story. With the ship now sailing, some of the children had become sea-sick, including Ellen and Margaret. They lay on their cots holding their queasy stomachs and when the nausea became too much, they leaned over the sides of their beds to vomit into a pail. Both girls spent the day in bed, only getting up to use the latrines.

After the first two days, Ellen and Margaret began to feel better and were able to get up and go explore the ship. Later in the day they found their way up to the top deck. Ellen noticed that this part of the ship was very different from the part where the children all stayed. Finely-dressed ladies strolled along the deck in beautiful evening gowns that shone like diamonds or floated like the down of a chick. Handsome men, wearing black suits and bow ties, escorted the ladies as they enjoyed the sea air.

"Oh, it's all so lovely," Margaret whispered, peering around the corner. Ellen thought they looked beautiful, too, as she crept to look through the dining room windows and saw couples dancing around and beautiful music floating through the air. Hiding behind a small screen, both girls were enchanted. Ellen thought she had never seen anything as wonderful in her entire life and she was right.

Life aboard the ship meant no chores, no one shouting at them or hitting them, and no one banging on their beds to wake them in the morning. Most of the children wished they could stay on the ship forever. Life for them had never been so good. All they had to do was sleep, eat and play.

It took two weeks to cross the ocean. As the ship approached shore the children stood by the railing, craning their necks to see the new land. They were told it was a place called Halifax. The wealthy passengers disembarked first and Ellen watched as they walked down the gangplank, the glamorous women wearing furs and silks, their children wrapped warmly in woolen coats. If they happened to glance at the children shivering in the cold in clothing too thin for a Canadian winter, they quickly looked away.

Finally, the children were assembled and marched off the ship.

"You will now go on trams to the new Hope House," the staff told them. "Be quiet and orderly. We want you to set a good example for the home."

Ellen looked at Margaret with raised eyebrows. After two weeks of freedom, it was over. "I hope the new place will be warm," she said. "I'm freezing."

As they had waited for the tram to come to take them to their new home, snow started to fall. Margaret blew on her hands and stamped her feet. "I can't feel my feet," she said. "And I'm really hungry. I wonder if we will get something to eat when we get there."

It took almost no time to get to the home from the docks. Standing at the front door they were surprised that this building was not large like the one in England had been, but long and low with lots of small windows.

Once inside, they found a large, open room with a fire roaring in a huge fireplace. The children rushed to its circle of warmth and huddled around it holding their hands out the flames and giggling with delight.

A young woman strode into the room. "Children, children," she called to them, "you may call me Miss Jane. I am in charge and I will take you to your dormitory then you will have something hot to eat and drink."

Hungry and tired, they scurried after her. Though she seemed nice, Ellen felt wary. Her experiences at her previous home had taught her that things were not always as they seemed.

The dormitory had been set up in the same way as the other home with cots in rows, about thirty on each side of the long room. By now Ellen knew the routine. She picked a cot nearest the door so she could be the first one out at meal time. Margaret jumped on the one next to her. Putting their bags in the cupboards, they waited for Miss Jane to take them to the dining room.

In the dining room, the quiet children waited for the food to arrive, tired and unsure of what to expect. When their plates landed in front of them they stared, not recognizing what they saw. There was something called sweet potato served with ham. Next came a bowl of hot macaroni with melted cheese which the staff served in large helpings. Ellen had never seen anything like it in her life. Hot sweet tea followed along with something called cookies. Ellen thought this a silly name since it really was only a biscuit.

After eating they were told to go to bed so Ellen and Margaret staggered to the dormitory and fell exhausted into their beds.

# Chapter Twenty-five

The days passed and the routine was much the same as it had been at her previous home but without the horrible Mrs. Shaw. While they all had lots of chores to do, the home had younger staff and the workers were much kinder to the children. Gradually the numbers of the children shrank as adopting families claimed them.

One day, Ellen was told that Matron had sent for her. Terrified, she ran to the office and tapped timidly on the door then waited until she heard someone call, "Enter."

The matron at this home was an older woman, very plump, and she wore glasses on the end of her nose. Peering at Ellen over their tops, she shuffled some papers on her desk.

"Well, Ellen, it seems we have found a family for you by the name of Mathews," she said. "You have a long journey on the train ahead of you and as it will take quite a few days to get there, a staff member will accompany you. Someone from the Mathews family will meet you when you arrive at your destination. You are fortunate to be placed so soon. I hope you will be a good girl and do well."

*At last,* Ellen thought, *someone wants me.* "Please, Miss," she said. "Am I to be adopted?"

"No Ellen, you are going there to help Mrs. Mathews. She has five children and cannot manage them all. The family has requested a girl from Hope House to come and live with them and help out around the house and farm.

Ellen was almost nine years old by now and even though life had been hard in the home, she was frightened to be leaving the only security she had known since her mother had given her away. Matron told her to get her things ready as she would leave the next day.

Back at the dormitory, Ellen found Margaret busy cleaning floors. Kneeling beside her, she said, "Matron says I'm going to a family tomorrow. I will have to leave you."

Margaret sat back on her heels, her face crumpling as great tears rolled down her cheeks. "I want to go with you," she said. "I thought we would stay together." They had been inseparable for almost two years and now felt like sisters. The two girls clung to each other and sobbed.

Early the next morning Ellen and five other girls climbed into a car that took them to the train station. Margaret didn't want to let Ellen go and begged Miss Jane to take her, too, but it was not to be. While Ellen watched through the car window, another staff member held onto Margaret.

At Ellen's last sight of her friend, Margaret stood sobbing, arms out, and pleading to go with her. Ellen waved until she could no longer see her friend then she slumped into the car seat and tried not to cry.

Once on the train she ran to get a window seat like the last time she had ridden on a train, only this time it was a much nicer train. It had soft, upholstered seats and blinds that Ellen pulled up and down until Miss Jane scolded her and told her to behave herself like a proper young lady. The other children asked a lot of questions about their new homes until they too were told to be quiet and read a book. At each city one more child left the train as a new family waited to collect her. Ellen watched with envy and hope as one little girl was greeted with hugs and kisses. Perhaps she would be so lucky.

After four days of travelling Ellen began to think that this trip would never end. Snow fell thick and deep and it was nearly dark when she finally received the command to collect her bag. Miss Jane led her into a small station where they were to greet Mr. Mathews. He was not there. Speaking to the station master, Miss Jane said, "I have this young child in my charge but I must to return to the train. Would I be able to leave her with you until Mr. Mathews arrives?"

Scratching his head, he looked at Ellen. "Well, I guess it will be all right," he said. She's mighty young to be left alone, don't you think?"

"Oh, I'm sure he will be here soon," Miss Jane replied. "We have a contract and he understands his responsibilities towards this child."

Bending down, she told Ellen, "You must wait in here until Mr. Mathews picks you up. I cannot stay any longer or I shall miss the train. I am sure he will not be long. Be a good girl, Ellen. I hope you like your new family." Taking Ellen to a seat near a pot-bellied stove, she squeezed her hand then walked out the door to the platform.

After an hour the station door burst open and a big man in a leather coat stood in the entrance glaring at her. He had a full, red beard, dark eyes that bore into her, and he wore a fur hat with ear flaps.

"Are you the girl from the home?" he shouted.

Gulping, Ellen jumped up. "Y-yes sir," she said.

"Come with me," he hollered. Nodding to the station master he turned and strode out the door leaving Ellen to collect her own bag and follow him out into the howling wind and blinding snow. Mr. Mathews' horse and cart waited on the road. Ellen threw her bag up then climbed up to the seat. Her thin coat was no defense against the cold temperatures and Mr. Mathews offered her no coverings.

"Are you Mr. Mathews?" Ellen asked.

He grunted a muttered complaint about coming out in such foul weather and snapped the horse's reins.

"I'm sorry, but would you have a blanket or something? I am so cold."

"No, I don't," he growled. "You'll have to toughen up if yer gonna live out here. I heard you English kids were soft. Why the wife wanted you, I don't know. It weren't my idea to get you so don't get in my way or you'll be sorry."

Ellen hunched her shoulders against the cold and hung on. The man did not speak to her again until the wagon pulled up in front of a run-down farm house with a pale light shining from the window through the snow.

"This is it," he announced. "Get down and grab yer bag. I have to stable the horse. Go on into the house and the wife will see to you."

Leaving her standing alone in the snow, he drove off. Ellen looked around. The place looked run down and shabby. She wanted to cry but instead she swallowed hard and hitched her bag up on her arm. Shoulders back, she knocked at the door. Immediately, it swung open and a small, tired-looking woman motioned her in.

The room was not very large. It had a stone floor and big brick fireplace in which hung a large iron pot full of what smelled like stew bubbling away over a wood fire. A few old chairs sat next to the fire and a wooden table stood in the centre of the room.

"You must be Ellen," the woman said. "My name is Norma. I hope the journey was not too bad for you. It is a long way you have come. Give me your coat and sit down and I'll get you something to eat. You must be starved by now."

Ellen nodded, encouraged by her kind words. "I am hungry and cold. My coat is so thin the wind blows right through it." She tried to smile but she felt so scared and alone she couldn't do it.

Norma took her to the chair by the fire and, sitting down opposite her, she said, "It must be very hard for you, my dear, being so far away from your home. I am not sure what they told you at Hope House. You are here to help me with the farm work and the children. I have five and it's all I can do to keep up. There is not enough room in the house for you, but I have made a nice little room for you over the barn. I am sure you will like it. I have put a small stove in there so you should be nice and warm."

After she had eaten, Ellen heard the sound of feet thumping down the stairs, a door burst open, and five children poured into the room.

"Is it okay to come down now, Ma?" one of them asked.

"Cor! Is she the girl from over the sea? She don't look any different than us," another said, sounding quite disappointed. *Did they expect her to have two heads*, Ellen wondered.

Norma hushed them. "This is Ellen," she explained. "She's here to help around the house." Lining them up, she said to Ellen, "This one is Tom. He's my eldest at ten, then Brian's almost nine, Nell seven, Amy almost six, and Peter only four."

Ellen looked at these children and thought of Sammy and Sarah, then pushed the memory of their faces out of her mind. *Well, at least they seem friendly,* she thought. *Maybe it won't be so bad here.*

After a while the children were ordered to get ready for bed. By now, Ellen could hardly keep her eyes open and Norma noticed and ushered her towards the door. Offering her a woolen blanket, she said, "Come with me, I will show you your room."

Bracing against the snow and wind once more, Ellen struggled after her carrying her bag. At the barn, Norma lit a lantern then went over to the bottom of a ladder and, signaling for Ellen to follow, climbed up through a hatch in the ceiling. Norma raised the lantern up so Ellen could see and Ellen looked around, pleasantly surprised to see a small comfortable room waiting for her. There was a bed, a little night stand, and wardrobe for her clothes. In the corner, a pot-bellied stove glowed making the room warm and snug and on the floor lay a handmade rag rug with many colours. The rug reminded her of the one her mother had made and she felt hot tears slide down her cold cheeks. She turned to Norma to thank her but was too choked-up to say anything.

Seeing the girl's sad face, Norma reached out and pulled Ellen into a hug. "Please don't cry," she said. "Everything will be okay. Just give it time. Tomorrow is a new day. I think you and I will get on well. I need the help, and you need a home, so you see, we need each other. When I leave, you can close the hatch. That will help keep your little room warm. I will tell you what your duties are tomorrow." Stroking Ellen's hair away from her face, she smiled and said, "Goodnight, little Ellen."

Life on the Mathews farm was arduous and

difficult. The small kindnesses that Norma tried to show to her were more than overshadowed once Mr. Mathews came into the room. A cruel man, he shouted and beat his wife if he found she had not followed his orders. The children fared no better and spent most of their time trying to stay out of his way. While the boys toiled in the fields, the girls fed and watered the animals. Only little Peter was allowed to play. Ellen knew that would not last.

Norma thought Ellen very mature for her age. She was a pretty child, and would be a beautiful young woman someday. Ellen seemed able to take on any task she was asked to do and Norma was glad to have help. She did not have time to give much thought to how Ellen coped with all the changes in her life.

Ellen started each day the same way, up early to draw water from the well. With no plumbing, some days the well was frozen solid and she would have to break through the ice with a long iron bar to draw water. After that she helped with breakfast then spent all day working, doing chores around the farm house. At the end of each day she fell into bed exhausted.

This was her life for the next three years.

# Chapter Twenty-six

By the time Ellen turned twelve years old her appearance had changed a lot. Since she had arrived at the Mathews' farm she had filled out and grown tall for her age. A pretty girl, she had light copper-coloured hair the same as her mother's, and when the sun shone on it, it seemed on fire. Like her mother, she had emerald green eyes and by now, she had developed small breasts.

Now Ed Mathews started to look at her differently. His sly glances made Ellen uncomfortable but she knew almost nothing about boys and men only that they were different from her. Norma had warned her not to let boys touch her but she didn't really know what that meant.

The contract with the Matthews' had stated that Ellen was to attend a small one-room school house two days a week. The school was mixed, younger and older children, boys and girls mostly from the surrounding farms. Though she loved to learn, she hated going to school because the local boys tormented her continually.

She was known as a "Home girl" and treated worse than the lowest person. She found it impossible to make friends and to fit in with the other children. Alone at night in her little room in the loft, Ellen often wondered what happened to her friend Margaret, the last real friend she had ever known. She had not seen or heard of her since she had left Hope House.

Each day that passed Ellen found it harder and harder to avoid Ed Mathews. He seemed to be around every corner no matter where she went as she did her chores. One day, Norma said, "Go pick some blackberries for baking then you can help me make pies."

Ellen took the pail and walked across the field to where the blackberry bushes grew abundant on the fence line. She started to gather them then turned to find Ed Mathews there, leering at her.

"You look mighty perty today, Ellen," he said, licking his lips and sidling closer.

She backed away but he lunged for her. She tried to turn and run but the heel of her boot caught on a blackberry bramble and she fell backwards. In an instant he flung himself on top of her, pinning her to the ground. Grabbing the front of her dress he ripped it away and began rubbing her breast and pinching her nipples. He tried to kiss her mouth, slobbering on her face as she wrenched away from his foul breath. He panted and groaned, in a frenzy to pull up her skirt. It seemed like his hands were all over her as he tried to rip of her underpants.

Ellen struggled and kicked, biting his face and leaving long scratches on his cheek. He let go of her for a second, howling in pain. She saw her chance to twist away and she heaved his sweaty body off her own and ran as fast as she could, not daring to look back.

She did not know what to do or where to go but knew there was only one place. She had to go to Norma and tell her what had happened. When Ellen crashed through the kitchen door, panting and dirty, Norma was shocked at the state of her. Gasping and crying, Ellen told her what had happened but Norma would not believe it. Shouting at Ellen, she said, "No. He would never do such a thing. He has his faults but not that." Screaming, she commanded Ellen to go to her room.

Before she could leave the house, Norma's husband came in with scratches on his face. He told her that Ellen had tried to tempt him and that he'd had to fight her off. Ellen knew that Norma didn't believe him but she also knew that because Norma was afraid of him and that her home and children were at stake if she confronted him it would be easier for her to blame Ellen.

"Tell those people at Hope House that they must take her back. She's a slut and out of control and we can't manage her," he commanded. "I want her gone as soon as possible." Norma only nodded.

Ellen sat in her room, sobbing. Why was this happening to her? She thought Norma would believe her but now she knew that there was no one whom she could trust.

A few weeks later word came from the home. They said they were very sorry the child had caused so much trouble and asked the Matthews' to put Ellen on a train and send her back. The intervening weeks had been excruciating for Ellen. Feeling guilty about her part in Ellen's abuse, Norma had ignored her and when she gave Ellen chores to do, she shouted at her and demanded more than Ellen could do. Ed Matthews was even worse. When his wife was not around he leered at Ellen, breathing down her collar and describing in lurid detail what he would do to her soon, all the while sniggering and rubbing his groin. Though the children were not aware of what had happened they did not like having Ellen at their home anymore because the other children at school teased them about her. So on a cold, bleak day Ed Mathews and his wife took Ellen back to the train station where she had arrived that first day and left her there alone to wait for the train.

She was relieved to be leaving such a miserable existence and secretly hoped she would finally be sent back to England and home.

# Chapter Twenty-seven

Ellen had received only a few letters from her mother while at the Mathews' farm. Since her mother was not allowed to have an address for Ellen, the letters had been forwarded from Hope House. These letters had been quite short, telling Ellen to be a good girl and not to get into trouble and that maybe she would be allowed to come home when she was older.

Mary had no idea of the terrible hardships and the kind of life Ellen had led since giving her up. Much later, Ellen was to discover that all her letters were screened by the home and had been censored. The only bit of information that Hope House allowed Ellen to find out was that her mother had remarried. The new husband's name was Charles Shipton. Ellen also found out that her mother had never given up Sam or Sarah.

When Ellen learned that only she had been given away, bitterness consumed her. At the time, she had been much too young to remember or understand her mother's struggle and she did not she realize that Hope House had lied about Ellen being able to go home any time her mother wished. Hurt and angry, Ellen decided to cut off all correspondence with her family.

"What's a young thing like you doin' travellin' all alone across the country?" the station master asked as she stood looking out at the leaden sky.

"What do you care?" Ellen replied.

"But you can't be more than ten years old, dearie," he said kindly. "You're about the same age as my granddaughter and I wouldn't be puttin' her on the train to go clear across the country alone."

"I'm twelve," Ellen said, swallowing back tears, "and I can take care of myself."

Her mother hadn't wanted her and the Matthews' had discarded her. Hope House had tricked her and even Norma, who she thought was a friend, had turned against her. Inside, she burned with resentment. She made her mind up that the only way she could protect herself was to never trust anyone again. Trusting always ended in pain.

Days later, Ellen arrived back at Hope House. Everything was the same as it had been when she left. Only the faces were new. She discovered, to her dismay that she was now considered a problem child and would therefore be difficult to place in another home. Convicted without trial or questioning, nothing she said made any difference; no one even wanted to hear her side of the story.

After a lot of persuading, the matron at Hope House had managed to find a place for her with a widow named Mrs. Sharp. The position promised to last only a short while as Mrs. Sharp just needed help while her daughter was away. Ellen was to be in service and would be paid a small wage which the home would keep in trust for her until she was older. She was surprised to hear she would receive any money at all since she had slaved for the Mathews' for the past three years for nothing.

The next day a carriage took Ellen to Mrs. Sharp's home. One of the staff from the home accompanied her, a stout, kindly lady named Doris. On the drive, Doris chatted away like she and Ellen had been friends for years and by the time they reached their destination, Ellen almost wished she could turn around and go back to the home with her.

# Chapter Twenty-eight

The carriage pulled up in front of a tall, brick house with a fancy, carved white door in the front. Doris rang the bell and Mrs. Sharp opened it herself. An elderly lady with a halo of white hair, she walked with a cane and smiled when she invited them into the wide hallway. Ellen thought that was a good sign. They followed Mrs. Sharp into a lovely, spacious living room. The walls, covered in pale yellow, flowered paper, glowed in the afternoon light. A crackling fire burned in the fireplace and a huge bouquet of roses sat on a large table in the centre of the room. Ellen thought it was the most beautiful place she had ever seen.

"This is our girl, Ellen," said Doris. "You'll find her a willing worker and a nice, quiet girl."

Mrs. Sharp took Ellen's hand and smiled sweetly. "I'm sure we will get along famously, shan't we, Ellen?" she said.

"Well, then," Doris said, giving Ellen a pat on the shoulder, "I must go as they will be expecting me back at the home."

Mrs. Sharp showed her out then shambled back into the room, leaning on her cane. "Are you hungry or thirsty, my dear?"

She could only nod her head in reply. No one had treated her so kindly for many years and Ellen was not used to being asked what she wanted.

"You follow me and we'll see what we can find." Mrs. Sharp led her to a cozy kitchen with a big oven range, a huge wooden table in the center, and pots and pans hanging from a rack suspended from the ceiling. A small bouquet of flowers tumbled from a vase on a sideboard against the wall and behind it stood rows of shelves filled with dishes, plates and platters.

Mrs. Sharp prepared a ham sandwich and a glass of milk for Ellen while she explained what her chores would be. "I need someone to do the general cleaning upstairs and down," she said, slathering butter on the bread. "I find it a little difficult now that I am getting older and my leg sometimes pains me. Do you think you could manage that?"

Ellen nodded, her mouth too full to speak. After the hard work of the farm, this sounded almost too easy. After Ellen finished her sandwich, Mrs. Sharp produced a plate of cookies and Ellen ate four of them as she drank the rest of her milk.

"I'll show you to your room now," Mrs. Sharp said, putting Ellen's dirty dishes into the sink and leaving them there. She took her up the stairs to a small room at the back of the house. A single bed with a pretty pink and white bedspread stood against one wall and a narrow cupboard for her clothes stood against another. A pink and blue carpet covered nearly the entire floor. The bathroom for her to use was at the end of the hall. Ellen could not believe such a beautiful room was all for her and, overwhelmed with emotion and gratitude, she turned to thank Mrs. Sharp but instead burst into tears. She sat on the edge of the pretty bed and sobbed.

"Whatever is wrong, my dear?" Mrs. Sharp cried, sitting beside Ellen and putting an arm around her shoulders. Ellen recounted the trials of her last position, the awful working conditions, the farmer's assault and the bullying at school.

"Oh, dear me," Mrs. Sharp crooned, hugging her again, "such terrible treatment and you just a child. You dry your eyes now. I promise that while you live under my roof you will never be treated like that again."

From then on, life for Ellen was better than it had ever been. Mrs. Sharp, good to her word, treated Ellen with kindness and Ellen worked hard to please her. Day by day, Ellen's confidence grew and her gratitude knew no bounds. For the first time since her mother had given her up to Hope House in England, Ellen began to feel safe. As the days passed, the old lady and the young girl grew closer and one day Mrs. Sharp suggested that Ellen call her by her first name, Beatrice.

"Oh, no, ma'am, I could never do that!"

In England such a thing would have been unheard of, but this country was not England and she realized that the people had dropped the confines of strict class distinctions.

"All right," Mrs. Sharp replied. "Why don't we compromise then? How does Miss Beatrice sound to you?"

Ellen's face broke into a wide smile. "Oh, Mrs. Sharp, that sounds wonderful. I mean, Miss Beatrice." With that she curtsied and went off to dust the banister.

Ellen had been with Miss Beatrice several weeks when the lady decided to arrange to keep her even after her daughter, Sylvia, returned. She couldn't bear the thought of throwing Ellen back into the kind of conditions that she had described and it broke he heart to see such a young child already so nervous and sad.

Compared to England, many things were very different in Canada. Ellen realized that people seemed to be much more equal and the class barrier that controlled everyone's lives in England sometimes did not even exist in this young country. She liked that, even though she still missed home very much. Sometimes in her bed at night she lay awake and looked out the window at the stars and wondered about her family. *Where were they now? Did they ever think about her?* Though she longed for the home that she had left behind, the bitterness she felt towards her mother continued to fester.

One day, after Ellen had been there four months, Miss Beatrice called Ellen into the sitting room. "Ah, there you are my dear," she said. "I wanted to let you know my daughter, Sylvia, is coming home soon. As you know, once she is back you were to return to the home but I have been very satisfied with your work here with me, Ellen, so I have been in touch with Hope House and arranged for you to stay here. Would you like that? I hope you will stay."

Ellen rushed to Miss Beatrice and threw her arms around her neck. "Oh, Miss Beatrice," she cried, "you do not know how much this means to me. I promise to work even harder for you." Thanking her again and again for her kindness, Ellen felt overwhelmed with happiness. She even felt the ice around her heart melt just a little. Someone actually wanted her. Fleetingly, she wondered if she would ever be allowed to go back home to England, but as things stood now she was not quite so anxious about that.

# Chapter Twenty-nine

The next few years went flew by for Ellen. At fifteen years old, she looked nothing like the nine year-old child who had stepped of that ship into the Canadian winter. She had developed the lovely figure of a young woman, with fiery copper-coloured hair in natural curls that cascaded down her back nearly to her waist. She didn't know she looked like her mother because all her memories had faded to pale images like old photographs. Living with Miss Beatrice and Sylvia had given her confidence like she had never had before. She and Sylvia had become good friends and she was happier than she had ever been. Sometimes she wondered about her family in England, but not often.

Occasionally, she received another letter from her mother and with encouragement from Miss Beatrice had decided to answer them. When she enquired about going home, her mother replied that she might be better off where she was and for once Ellen thought she was right. Ellen did not feel her mother wished her to return home and assumed that she was still unwanted. What she did not realize was that her mother was afraid to see Ellen again. She had never been able to forgive herself for giving her daughter away.

Miss Beatrice liked to entertain her friends in the afternoons and one day Ellen caught the eye of Vincent, the son of Miss Beatrice's bridge partner, Mrs. Scott. Vincent's mother often came to visit Miss Beatrice and he sometimes accompanied her.

"Your hair is so pretty," he said one day after following Ellen into the kitchen. He reached out and twirled a lock between his fingers, sliding up to her so that she could feel the heat of his body. Ellen felt a blush rise up all the way from her toes. She stepped away from him but he moved with her, this time coming even closer. "We should spend more time together," he said, his voice like thick cream.

Ellen had been warned about the opposite sex and the memory of her experience with Ed Matthews filled her with trepidation.

"You're so pretty," cooed Vincent, stroking her cheek with the side of his thumb. He loved the thrill of conquest and this little morsel of feminine sweetness was too good to pass up, he thought.

Vincent fancied himself quite a ladies' man and now he had found his next delightful little distraction.

More and more, he found ways to be alone with her whenever he brought his mother to visit and each time he pressed himself closer to her, brushing her arm or touching her hand. In spite of her misgivings, Ellen found herself falling under his spell.

Miss Beatrice noticed what was happening. She warned Ellen not to take Vincent seriously. "You are much too young for him, my dear. You have to be careful about ones like that. They are only after one thing."

Ellen had no idea what that one thing was, but she found that she didn't care. She thought about Vincent night and day and looked forward to seeing him every chance she could get. She wanted to heed Miss Beatrice's warnings but the next time Ellen saw Vincent and he asked her if she would like to go for a walk she told him what Miss Beatrice had said. He laughed. "I would never take advantage of you," he told her. "I respect you far too much."

Ellen, flattered by his protestations, secretly arranged to meet him the next day. She could hardly concentrate on her chores all day as she watched the hands on the clock move ever so slowly. That night she found it hard to sleep, just thinking about how wonderful it would be to see him tomorrow as soon as she had finished her duties. She asked Miss Beatrice if it would be all right for her to go for a walk knowing that she would assume that Ellen would be alone. Ellen felt bad about deceiving Miss Beatrice but her desire to see Vincent overshadowed any guilt she suffered.

Ellen put on her shawl and ran out the back door and down the lane toward the park where Vincent had arranged to meet her. When she arrived at the site of their planned assignation, she looked around but could not see him anywhere. A pang stabbed her heart. He would not come and she would be tricked again, she thought, glancing around but just when she was about to turn toward home, head hanging, he stepped out from behind a tree.

"Oh, Vincent," she sighed. "I thought you had deserted me."

He put his arm around her, kissed her cheek and said, "Never, my sweet. How could I leave a beauty like you?"

Ellen's heart beat so fast she thought she might faint. Her first kiss! And it felt so wonderful, more wonderful than she had ever imagined. She hoped he would kiss her again.

Vincent did not disappoint. He took her hand and strolled to a secluded place in the park then pulled her behind the lilac bushes and held her in his arms. His lips descended on hers and he kissed her passionately.

Ellen felt like she was drowning but found it impossible to resist him. Vincent he kissed her neck, making Ellen gasp and awakening delicious new sensations that she had never experienced before then suddenly he stopped and pushed her gently away. "I'm taking you home before I forget I am a gentleman," he said, laughing softly. Ellen didn't know that Vincent lived by his own motto where women were concerned: Always leave them wanting more.

Ellen felt sure he loved her as much as she loved him. He was so caring and considerate. As they walked hand in hand back home she felt like she had clouds beneath her feet and everything around her sparkled.

"When can I see you again?" Vincent asked as they walked up the stairs to the back door.

"I don't know," Ellen replied. "Miss Beatrice doesn't wish me to see you."

"But we're in love. We have to be together."

"I will find a way," Ellen promised, standing on her tiptoes and kissing him one more time.

Ellen managed to meet him several times a week, sneaking out while Miss Beatrice read by the fire in the evening or on her afternoons off work. Vincent started taking her to his friend's apartment so they could have more privacy, a tactic he often used while in pursuit of his latest conquest. Before long they became lovers as Vincent inveigled his way into Ellen's affections. He managed to convince her that intimacy was all part of falling in love and that he would marry her as soon as she was old enough. So convincing was he that she trusted him completely, the thrill of first love making her blind to his insincerity.

# Chapter Thirty

After a few months Ellen noticed Vincent seemed to become cool towards her and a few times he did not show up when a meeting had been arranged. She also began to feel sick in the morning, sometimes even vomiting before breakfast. She knew very little about her own body but she realized that something had changed. Ellen remembered some details that Norma had described to her about her own pregnancies and now she was terrified that she might be pregnant herself because the symptoms were the same. She planned to tell Vincent about her fears the next time they were together so they could make plans to marry right away. He would do the right thing and take care of her, she was sure of it.

She hurried to meet him and waited on the park bench at the arranged time. She waited until long after he had promised to see her but still he did not show up. After a while, a small boy approached and handed her a message. She tore open the envelope with trembling fingers and as her eyes scanned his writing, they filled with tears. The letter read,

*Ellen.*

*I'm going away for a while. I'm sorry to end it this way. I do not see any future for us. It was fun while it lasted but this is for the best. I hope you will not think ill of me. I wish you well.*

*Vincent*

Ellen crumpled the note and jammed it into her pocket then turned toward home, her eyes filled with tears. She had loved him yet once again she had been used and tossed aside. Once she had vowed never to trust anyone but she had let down the barrier and now she had to admit that she had been taken advantage of again. She trudged home leaving a trail of pieces of her broken heart behind her. Whatever should she do now?

Miss Beatrice had noticed the change in Ellen over the past few weeks. Dark shadows circled her eyes and she went through her days as if in a trance. Miss Beatrice could not understand why Ellen now seemed so unhappy. Calling her to the living room one afternoon, she asked "Is anything worrying you, Ellen? I am concerned about you. Can I help in any way?"

Ellen knew she couldn't keep her secret any longer. "Oh, Miss Beatrice, I am so ashamed," she cried, wringing her hands. The whole story spilled out of her; the clandestine meetings, the love affair with Vincent, his betrayal. "Now I think I might be pregnant," she sobbed.

Miss Beatrice pressed her lips together and said nothing for what seemed a long time. Ellen read the look on her face and, filled with remorse for deceiving this wonderful woman who had been so kind to her, wept all the harder. She knew there was nothing she could say or do that would make things right, and there was nothing she could do now but wait and see what was going to happen.

Finally, Miss Beatrice spoke in a tight voice. "Ellen, I am shocked and disappointed with your behaviour, especially considering that I warned you about Vincent. His kind preys on innocent young girls. But clearly, you did not listen to me. Go to your room now. I will speak with you later."

Twilight had descended by the time Miss Beatrice knocked on Ellen's door.

"Come in," said Ellen, in a tiny voice.

Miss Beatrice pushed open the door but did not enter. "I have been in touch with Hope House," she said. "I want you to leave as soon as possible. I cannot put into words how disappointed I am in you, Ellen. I feel that you have let me down and I do not want you in my home anymore."

Ellen gasped and covered her face with her hands. *It couldn't be true,* she thought. She never for a moment believed that Miss Beatrice would send her away. She had always been so sympathetic and understanding, so willing to help her. She actually believed that this woman loved her.

"Oh, Miss Beatrice, please don't send me away" she cried, looking up. But there was no one there.

Ellen did not consider how hurt and upset Miss Beatrice felt over her flagrant disregard for her warnings about Vincent. She sat on the bed looking at the lovely room and weeping. She hated to leave the one place where she had felt happy. She didn't know what she would do about having a baby, but she did know that she would never go back to Hope House in disgrace. Later that evening, when the house was quiet, she packed a few of her things in a bag and crept out into the night. She did not have any idea where she would go but knew she needed to get as far away as she could.

Stuffing the small amount of cash that Miss Beatrice had given her over the years into her handbag, she headed for the train station. It would not be difficult to disappear in a country the size of Canada.

# Chapter Thirty-one

The only train leaving that night was for the city of Toronto. She had just enough money for a ticket with a little left over. With so little money, she would have to be extremely careful and would need to find work right away. She could not think about the baby she was carrying right now. Her first goal had to be to find somewhere to live then find work. And she had to do it all by herself.

She found a seat on the train and stowed her bag on the rack overheard. Looking out into the black night she suddenly felt overwhelmed by everything that had happened to her. Tears slid from the corners of her eyes and rolled down her cheeks without Ellen even being aware that she was crying. A quivering knot of fear lurked under her breastbone.

From the seat across the aisle, a young woman watched her. She wondered what a pretty young girl was doing travelling all alone at night. When she noticed the tears, she got out of her seat and sat down next to Ellen. "Hello, I'm Katie," said the round blonde girl with a splash of freckles over her nose. She did not mention the tears nor ask what caused them. "Where are you heading? Are you alone?"

Ellen mopped her face with a balled up handkerchief and answered, yes, she was alone. "My name is Ellen," she said, sniffing, "and I'm not sure where to go once I get off the train." She explained to Katie that she had to leave her last place of employment quite suddenly but did not explain why. It felt good to have someone to talk to and Katie seemed genuinely friendly. The train rattled through the night as the two struck up a conversation and found they liked each other's company.

"I have a small place of my own," Katie told Ellen. "You're welcome to come and stay with me until you get things sorted out."

"Oh, could I really?" Ellen cried. "That would help me so much. It won't be for long, I promise. I plan to find a job right away. I don't know how to thank you."

A few hours later Katie announced that it was time to collect their bags as they would be arriving soon. At the station they went out into the night air and ran for the tram, breathless and laughing. It felt so good to Ellen to have something to laugh about again and to forget her worries if even just for a little while.

"Time to get off the tram now," Katie said a few minutes later as she picked up her bag. "From here it's only a short walk to my place."

They climbed the stairs along the side of an old, brick building and Katie turned her key in the lock and pushed the door open. The apartment had a tiny kitchen and a small living room with one window. Katie explained, "You will have to sleep on the couch since there is only one bedroom with a small bed and that's definitely mine." Ellen readily agreed. She would have agreed to almost anything that night to avoid having to sleep on a train station bench or in a shop doorway.

After washing and saying goodnight, Ellen crawled between the blankets that Katie had spread out for her on the couch. Pulling them up under her chin she stared up at the patterns that the streetlights cast on the ceiling. This was the first time she had been offered kindness without anything expected in return. Even Miss Beatrice's kindness came with conditions but Ellen had never had a true friend since Margaret. She hoped Katie's kindness came with no strings attached.

The next morning, Ellen woke before Katie and lay on her side looking at the room. Katie's mad idea of decorating and color left Ellen speechless. With bright blue on one wall, red on another, a dazzling splash of yellow on a third and an orange ceiling, it was certainly a happy room. Two worn but comfortable-looking chairs nudged the arms of the sofa. A tiny table and two wooden chairs, painted red, sat in the kitchen against a tiny window that looked out onto a brick wall. Even in this riot of colour in a stranger's apartment, Ellen had a feeling of home.

# Chapter Thirty-two

Ellen knew that the first thing she needed to do was to find work so she could pay for her keep and find her own place. She couldn't live with Katie forever, in fact, Katie might want her to leave tomorrow for all she knew.

That day, with Katie's help and directions, Ellen went in search of a job. First, she tried the factories nearby but no one was hiring. Every day she went out and trudged the streets of the city as far as her aching feet would take her and found nothing then one day she noticed a small help-wanted sign in the window of a florist's shop. The only experience she had with flowers was occasionally arranging bouquets for Miss Beatrice, but she went in to apply anyway.

After a short interview with the owner, a tall, balding man named Mr. Wainwright, he agreed to give her a chance on a month's trial. "Report for work tomorrow morning at seven," he instructed, shaking Ellen's hand.

Ellen skipped all the way home to Katie's apartment. She would receive training on the job and she could hardly wait to get started. If things worked out she would be able to provide a home for herself and her baby.

She did not want to think about the pregnancy, but she had already begun to notice how her belly had rounded and it wouldn't be long until it became obvious to others as well. The first person she must tell about the baby was Katie.

That evening after they had eaten and sat drinking a cup of tea, Ellen said, "Katie, I have something I have to tell you." Katie set down her teacup. "I'm going to have a baby," Ellen said, hanging her head. She explained to Katie about what had happened with Vincent and how he had tricked and used her even though he had led her to believe that he had been in love with her. She described how Miss Beatrice had reacted to the news of her pregnancy and forced her to leave, planning to send Ellen back to Hope House. She even revealed how Ed Matthews had molested her and Norma had turned against her. Once again, Ellen's face was wet with tears.

Katie reached across the table and squeezed Ellen's hand. "I already suspected something was up," she said. "I can see that bump under your dress and figured out that there was a story behind it somewhere. I just thought I should wait until you were good and ready to talk about it."

With Katie's encouragement Ellen went on to tell her about how her mother had abandoned her and how she ended up in Canada. Katie seemed to genuinely care and offered no judgment. That night Ellen slept peacefully for the first time in a long time.

Katie suggested Ellen buy a cheap wedding ring and tell people that she had been widowed. They both knew that she would be held in contempt if it came out that she was not married and that her baby was illegitimate.

The next day, Ellen started her new job with a happy heart. She and Katie had agreed she should not mention anything about the baby until it became absolutely necessary. When she went to work she tied her apron loosely around her middle so that the bulge hardly showed.

Ellen took to her work with a natural talent and flare for design. Before long, she took over creating the elaborate arrangements ordered by fancy hotels and society weddings. Mr. Wainwright, delighted with her work, was also aware that her beauty and sweet, shy nature was proving an asset to his business. Customers liked her and many began asking to have Ellen to create their arrangements for them.

At five months into her pregnancy Ellen thought she owed it to her boss to tell him about the baby. He smiled. "I guessed as much." Believing her story about being a widow, he had never asked for details but now he inquired what she planned to do about her job once the baby came. He had become quite dependent on her skills. "I would like you to continue to work here after your baby is born if you think that is possible," he said, taking her hands in his.

"I would like that very much," she replied, gently pulling her hands away. "I don't know yet how I will manage, but I know I'll think of something and I do need the job."

That evening she talked things over with Katie and the two of them decided what they would do once the baby arrived. "First of all," Katie said, "I want you to know that I would like you to keep living here with me. We already know that we get along well together and with my health the way it is, the extra income helps when I am not able to work some days. I think that we can share the task of child minding, too," Katie offered. "I usually work evenings anyway, and I can hardly wait to get my hands on that little one. I love babies. When we both have to work we can ask Marion from next door if she will take your little one in with that brood of hers."

Ellen continued working until it was no longer possible to stand all day. Her feet swelled and her back ached from reaching past her huge belly to work at the flower counter. Mr. Wainwright fussed about her; he bought her a stool to sit on while she worked, but the day came when she was simply too tired to work and had to give in and stay home.

With only a few weeks to go until her due date, Ellen spent her days reading books from the library and occasionally taking the bus downtown to pick through the second hand shops looking for baby clothes. She realized that she wanted this baby very much and could not understand how her own mother had ever been able to give her away. She brought home an old wooden cradle and scrubbed it clean then pressed a down-filled pillow into its bottom for a mattress to cuddle her little infant. She washed, ironed and mended the used baby clothes that she had bought for pennies and arranged them in the drawer of a dresser that she and Katie had found abandoned down the alley.

# Chapter Thirty-three

In the early hours of one morning, Ellen woke with a cramp across her lower belly. In the silence of the night she stared up at the flickering stars and waited for another cramp. In quick succession, it was followed by more as stronger pains gripped her. She rolled off her bed on the couch and called Katie to tell her the baby was coming. When she stood up to go to the bathroom her water broke and gushed down her leg like a warm river. Katie leapt out of bed and rushed around the apartment, demented with excitement.

"You just sit there and wait," Katie said, throwing a shawl at Ellen. "I'm going to get Norman." A friend had offered to take them to the hospital in his delivery van when the time came. She ran out the door to alert their neighbour, wearing only her pyjamas and slippers, hair flying.

Twelve difficult, painful hours later, Ellen's precious, first-born boy emerged into the world, wrinkled and squawking. Ellen held him and stroked the pale, downy hair on his small head, examining every part of him. His skin, as soft as a rose petal soon turned pink and he surveyed his mother's face with a serious expression. Ellen thought he was the most adorable and perfect baby she had ever seen and she felt consumed with love for him.

She gazed in wonder at the new little life she had created. "I think I will call you Robert," she crooned. "It's a good, strong name." The baby gave a little grunt. "We're in agreement, then," she said. "Robert it is."

She stroked his soft cheek as he latched onto her breast with his pink mouth and she thought about her own mother, and felt a familiar stab of pain. She pulled Robert closer to her body. She could not even imagine ever letting him go.

Later that morning, Katie came rushing down the ward, her face red and glowing. "Oh, Ellen," she cried, "let me hold him. He's gorgeous."

The baby had been sleeping but Katie gathered him up in her arms and held him close. "What are you calling him?" she asked, kissing his head. Ellen told her that she had chosen the name Robert and Katie agreed that it suited him, so it was decided.

The next week Ellen took Robert home. He turned out to be a contented, quiet baby, always happy to be held in someone's arms, and with his Aunty Katie around that turned out to be most of the time. As time went, by little Robbie became the centre of Ellen's and Katie's world, and between the two of them, they managed his care with only the occasional help of a willing neighbor.

One day when Robbie was three months old, Katie hobbled home, bent nearly double. She had always suffered a weak back as a result of a childhood injury and had been finding it difficult to hold a job because she had to take frequent breaks to sit or lie down. Ellen's salary had increased continually since she had started working, so they decided that Katie should stay home full-time and take care of Robbie and the home. This suited Katie just fine as she adored little Robbie and was well-suited to taking care of him and the housekeeping.

In the time since Ellen had started working at the flower shop the business had doubled because of her abilities. Her boss knew that he could not manage to run the business now without her. Her floral designs were much sought after and her reputation had grown with the society ladies of the city who vied to show off the most elegant flower arrangements at their soirees.

Mr. Wainwright left her in charge most of the time and as he was becoming quite elderly it did not come as a surprise when one day he approached her and said, "Ellen, you know that I'm getting old and I don't want to work anymore. I want to do a little travelling while I still can and spend more time with my grandchildren before I die. I have decided to sell the shop and I want to give you the first opportunity to buy the business. You can think about it, but it would be a great opportunity for you."

Ellen had already considered what she would do if she had a chance to buy the flower business. "We will miss you when you go," she answered, "but I have been expecting this. I am definitely interested in purchasing the business. I will have to see about securing a loan."

At home that evening she discussed the offer with Katie. Her friend was almost more excited about the opportunity for Ellen than Ellen was herself and had no doubts about her ability to succeed. "Do not hesitate," she advised. "Take the chance to be your own boss."

Ellen knew she wanted to take every opportunity she could to succeed and provide for Robbie. She also had a burning desire to prove to everyone who had hurt her over the years that she did not need them. The only people she cared about now were her son and her dear friend Katie.

The next day she sought out Mr. Wainwright. "I have decided to take you up on your offer to buy the shop," she told him, "if you are sure you want to sell it to me. Thank you for giving me this opportunity."

His face lit up. "I am so pleased, Ellen," he said. "I cannot think of anyone else I would rather take over my business and I am sure you will be a huge success." Reaching out, he shook her hand. "There! We have a deal."

In a few short weeks everything legally transferred to Ellen's ownership. She felt excited and nervous at the same time. Looking forward to the challenges ahead, she felt confident that this was what she was meant to do. Everything had fallen into place quickly and easily. Under her direction, the business continued to prosper and for the first time Ellen felt in control of her own life.

# Chapter Thirty-four

Ellen was now only nineteen years old. She had grown into a beautiful young woman and had no idea how much she looked like her mother. Her life in England had become a faint memory.

Wherever Ellen went, she turned heads and she had many would-be suitors vying for her attention but brushed them all off. She had no interest in ever getting involved with a man again. Her experience with Vincent had left her bitter and cold towards any thought of romantic love.

In time, Ellen found that she and Robbie were able to move into a larger home. It was not unusual for two single women to live together and help each other, so it was agreed that Katie must move with them and continue to care for Robbie while Ellen worked. Ellen had noticed a house she liked while on her way to the shop one day. It had been empty for some time and sat neglected and forsaken. She made an appointment with the agent to view the property. Katie came to look at the house with her and Robbie tagged along holding Katie's hand. The moment they walked through the front door, they knew that this was the place for them.

A large living room stood to the right of the front door. It was in a sad state of repair but they could see its potential. To the left a once elegant dining room with exquisite moldings and hardwood floors now languished under a thick layer of dust. Robbie ran from room to room, calling, "My new house, my new house," as the two women excitedly explored. The agent told Ellen that there was a good school nearby where Robbie could attend once he was old enough.

"Oh, Ellen, it's perfect," Katie cried. "Once we decorate it, it will be the prettiest house."

Ellen smiled at Katie. "You are a natural born homemaker," she said, "and if you could get your flamboyant decorating under control, everything would be perfect."

The three of them moved into Ellen's new home and the flower shop business continued to grow. Ellen looked forward to a bright future for Robbie. In a few years, he would be starting school and Katie planned to get a part-time job once her day-time hours had been freed up again.

One morning in early fall, Katie dressed Robbie in his new coat and boots and headed out to buy some groceries for dinner that night. After visiting several shops, Katie clutched Robbie's hand as she stepped off the curb to cross a busy street. Her heel caught on the edge of the sidewalk and she tripped, dropping her shopping basket and spilling its contents. A jar of pickles smashed on the pavement and lettuce, apples, and cans rolled out into the road. A team of horses pulling a beer wagon had come down the street at a brisk trot and when the glass jar shattered, the horses spooked. Rearing up, eyes wild, they leapt forward and veered wildly. The driver fought with the reins but before he could regain control of the horses, the wagon tilted onto two wheels. The barrels of beer rolled, unbalancing the transport and it reeled over, right where Katie stood. She watched in horror as the barrels tumbled toward her and, in a flash, threw herself over Robbie to protect him. The wagon struck her full on with all the weight of its load, crushing both of them. As the horses sprinted forward, Katie's coat caught and her body was dragged along under the wagon until two men rushed out to grasp the horses' harness and stop them.

Someone screamed and passersby rushed to help the woman and the little boy lying in the street. A

189

man in a dark suit pushed the crowd back. "I'm a doctor. Let me through," he commanded, kneeling on the pavement next to Robbie's still body. For several minutes he tried in vain to revive the little boy before finally giving up. "It's no use," he said. "I'm afraid he's dead."

A collective gasp went up from the gathered crowd then a woman grabbed the doctor's sleeve and cried, "You must come to her," she said, pointing to where Katie lay still on the bloodstained pavement. "She needs help."

After a quick examination, the doctor shook his head, stood up and ran a hand across his forehead. "I'm sorry," he said. "She's gone, too."

## Chapter Thirty-five

Ellen stood in her shop going over the details of a large order for a wedding to take place the following week when the bell over the shop's door tinkled. Two policemen walked in. She looked up and smiled. "Can I help you?" she asked politely. Both officers removed their hats and a chill went through Ellen's body.

"Are you Mrs. Ellen Clarke?" the officer on the right asked. Ellen nodded, with fear rising like a wave through her entire being.

"May we speak with you in private, ma'am?"

Ellen led them to her small office in the back of the shop and sent her two apprentices up front to take care of incoming customers. She leaned against her desk, her fingers gripping the edge. "What's this about?" she asked, searching the policemen's faces.

"I'm afraid we have some bad news, Mrs. Clarke; very bad news." One of the officers told her what had happened.

Ellen's knees buckled and he caught her by the arm. "I don't understand," she said, shaking her head. "How could this be?"

"If you would be able to come with us to identify the bodies, ma'am, we think it would help."

"Yes, of course," Ellen answered in a daze of shock.

She went with the police to identify the bodies of the two most important people in her life. At the morgue, she found her precious Robbie lying cold and still on a slab with hardly a scratch on his tender cheek. She stood for a long time stroking his face with tears coursing down her own. How would she be able to carry on without her beautiful child, to know she would never hold him and cuddle him at night, and kiss away his tears? Finally, she whispered, "Rest well, my angel," and was led to where Katie's body lay. She had been told Katie had thrown herself over Robbie to protect him from the falling wagon and had been dragged a good distance by the runaway horses so her pretty face was disfigured by scrapes and gashes. When they pulled back the sheet to reveal the damaged body, all she saw was how her dearest friend had made the ultimate sacrifice to save Ellen's son. She touched a silken strand of Katie's pale hair and, kissing her own fingertip, she transferred her good-bye kiss to

Katie's torn cheek, thanking her friend forever for her loyalty and love.

The funerals were held a few days later. Many friends, neighbours, and customers turned out to pay their respects, amazing Ellen with their kindness. She had not realized how many friends she had made through her years in business. Many of them had also known Katie and Robbie from times when they had met in the flower shop.

Somehow Ellen managed to get through that dreadful day. Someone, she could not remember who, gave her a ride back to her house where the ladies in her neighbourhood and her staff had put on a small reception. It was all Ellen could do to remain standing until the gathering ended.

After they had all left she went straight to bed and allowed her intense grief to flow out in great, wracking sobs that felt like they would tear her apart. She did not know how she would carry on one more day.

For the next several weeks, Ellen moved through her life in a fog of suffering. Reminders of Katie and Robbie were everywhere. When she woke in the morning, she thought she heard Robbie's giggle as he ran into her room trying to wriggle up on her bed. But he never came. She pictured Katie going about her day and could see her in the kitchen or hear her singing her funny little songs to Robbie.

Ellen's business began to suffer. At first, her customers dropped by to offer words of comfort but little by little they dropped away, no longer able to look into Ellen's grief-stricken face.

One cold, winter day when Ellen decided to go for a walk in a nearby park, she sat on a bench and, pulling her knitted cap down over her ears, watched the snow drift across the frozen ground. It felt just like her heart, she thought, lonely and frozen. It was then she realized that there was now no reason for her to stay here; there was nothing left for her in Canada. She began to think about the family in England that she had left behind so many years before. Where were they now? Did they ever wonder about her? Since losing her child she felt empty and lost. She suddenly became aware that she needed to connect with someone, someone who might care for her if only a little. *Why not her own family?* she thought, a flicker of hope igniting within her.

Perhaps it was time to go back to England and see her mother again. By now her brother Sammy would be grown up and her little sister Sarah, a young lady. She would go back to England. She would try to find her mother again, to try to discover why her mother had given her up for adoption. The pain of losing Robbie made it even more impossible for her to understand how her mother could have done it. Suddenly, she had something to give her life a purpose. She had to know why she had been abandoned.

Ellen returned to the shop with one thought in mind, to earn enough money for her passage to England. She knew it would take some time since most of her money was currently tied up in the business and she had a sizable bank loan to pay back. It would be a while before the shop was in a good position to sell. She threw herself into working all the hours she could, building the business back up. She also found that working helped to deaden the pain. She adopted a pleasant, almost happy, demeanor and contacted all her former customers and invited them back to do business with her shop. Most of them were pleased to return.

She moved out of her big house, into a small apartment in order to cut her personal expenses and saved every penny she could. The house had seemed too large and much too empty with her there alone anyway, and everything reminded her of her great losses. She felt so very lonely without her son and her friend, Katie. The other friends she had made over the years tried to spend time with her and extend comfort, but Ellen gently refused all offers.

She lost weight because she often forgot to eat. Able to lose herself in the beautiful world of flowers, hours went by as she worked and it was only when she started to feel weak from hunger that she would nibble a few bites of something then go back to work. After twelve months she felt it was time to make her move.

Approaching an agent to help her sell her shop, Ellen was surprised to find there was a lot of interest, and a buyer showed up almost immediately, keen to take over the business as soon as Ellen could move on.

A deal was struck and Ellen, happy to sell so quickly, purchased her ticket to England, sold her belongings, and packed her bags.

# Chapter Thirty-six

Late in the fall, with the leaves along the St. Lawrence Seaway burnished in shades of red and gold, Ellen stood on the deck of the ship that would take her back to where her journey had begun. Watching the hustle and bustle all around her, her thoughts drifted back to her good-bye visit to the graves of Robbie and Katie.

Standing at Katie's grave, she had said, "Thank-you for being such a true friend to me for all those years. I know I do not need to ask you to take care of my beloved Robbie. I leave him in your care, until we meet again."

Her last words to Robbie were, "You were a wonderful son, my darling, and the light of my life. I miss you so much. I looked forward to seeing you grow into a handsome, strong man, but it was not to be. Even though you can't be with me, it is a comfort to know you are in a better place and I will see you again someday. Stay close to your Aunty Katie until it is my time to join you then we shall be together forever."

As Ellen watched the coastline of Canada slowly drift past, she wondered what her life would be like in a country she hardly remembered. She also wondered if she ever found her mother how she would be received. Time would tell.

On a cold, dreary day, Ellen arrived at the Liverpool docks and walked down the gangplank onto English soil again. She had no idea where to start her search for her family. The only thing she remembered was that she had come from a place called Birmingham. She decided that she would begin there. But first, she had to find somewhere to stay the night in Liverpool. She asked a porter if he could direct her to the nearest hotel or bed and breakfast.

Pushing his cap back, he scratched his head. "Well, there's plenty to choose from round here, ma'am," he said, "but my choice for a lady like you would be old Ma Murphy's. She keeps a clean house and cooks a decent breakfast. You won't go wrong with her place, love." Giving her directions to the house, he told her, "Don't worry about this 'ere case, dearie. I lives right next door to 'er and I can bring it back with me. I'll be up there soon."

Ellen was surprised how friendly the people

were; the ones she had met on the ship and even here at the docks. Making her way to the bed and breakfast, she knocked on the door of Number 21, as instructed. From the outside, it looked a neat, tidy house and stood on a street lined with similar-looking houses in a nice respectable neighborhood.

An old lady answered the door. "Hello love," she said, her wizened face lighting up with a toothy grin. "What can I do for you?"

"I hope you have a room available," she answered. "A young man at the docks, a porter, said he will bring my suitcase here on his way home from work."

She gave a chuckle. "Oh, that will be young Scotty. He's a treasure, to be sure. Your stuff will be quite safe with him. Come in, Ducks" she said. "As it happens, I do have a room and I'll show it to you." Leading the way, she said, "My name is Susan Murphy. Who might you be, then, my dear?"

Ellen introduced herself and Susan showed her to a small, comfortable room with only a bed and a wardrobe for her clothes. It was decorated in lovely pink fittings; in fact, pink was everywhere – the pink-striped curtains, the bedspread with a pattern of pink roses, and a pink rug on the floor. *Definitely not a man's room*, Ellen thought, concealing a smile.

Susan invited her to join her for a cup of tea.

"And maybe a bite to eat," she said. "You must be hungry after your journey." She showed her to a small cozy living room stuffed beyond its limits with big comfortable chairs. "Make yourself comfy, lass," she said. Susan had a table already set and, adding bread, butter and jam, invited Ellen to sit with her while she chattered away like an old friend.

Soon, after a little of encouragement, Ellen briefly shared with Susan where she had travelled from and why. Susan listened intently to Ellen's story. "Oh, you poor girl," she said, squeezing Ellen's hand after learning about the tragic deaths of Katie and Robbie. "To have experienced so much, so young; it's just not fair, is it, love?"

Ellen went on to tell Susan about her mission to find her long-lost family. Susan's face lit up. "My son and his wife live in Birmingham," she said. "I can give you their address if you like, so that if you need a place to stay, you can go there. I'm sure they will make you very welcome."

Ellen was moved by Susan's willingness to help. Just then a knock sounded on the front door and Susan hurried to answer it.

"There you are, Scotty," she said. "We wondered what had happened to Ellen's bags. I was beginning to think you'd taken a fancy to them," she joked.

"Not me, Ma," he replied. "I suppose you fixed the little lady up for the night. She looked pretty tired when she stepped off that ship. I thought your place would suit her because it's nice and quiet."

"Too right," Susan said. "And thanks for bringing the bags. I'll let her know you've been. Tara, love."

Early the next morning after eating a full, English breakfast of eggs, sausage, and fried bread Ellen thanked Susan for her help, then paid her and set off on her search for her mother. She thought if she could locate Hope House, it might be the best place to start looking as they would surely have her mother's address in their records.

Catching a train to Birmingham, Ellen realized she was looking forward to this new part of her life with a mixture of excitement and trepidation. *Maybe I'll finally feel a sense of belonging somewhere,* she thought. *Maybe I will finally have my family back.*

When Ellen arrived in Birmingham, it did not take long to find her way to Hope House. She stepped into a butcher shop and asked for directions.

"It's not far, love," the rotund butcher replied. "Just hop on the tram at the corner and the driver will tell you where to change." He pointed up the street with his cleaver.

Before long, Ellen found herself standing at the same gates where she had stood so many years before looking in and expecting an exciting new life to begin. How different it had all turned out. Clutching a bar on the cold, wrought-iron gate, Ellen struggled for breath as the memories of that awful day came flooding back. She had been torn from her mother's arms and thrust into a cold unfeeling world. Her heart recalled all the despair and all the fear. All those terrible emotions threatened to drown her once more in utter hopelessness. For so many years, she had managed to submerge them, hiding the pain deep within her soul but now they rose up to consume her.

Taking a deep breath, she pushed open the gates and forced her legs to carry her forward. She knew if she was ever going to understand her own past, she had to take these steps. Walking up to the big house, she pulled on the bell rope.

# Chapter Thirty-seven

The door creaked open and a little girl about seven years old stood looking up at Ellen. Ellen smiled at her and asked if she could see Matron.

The girl bobbed and said, "Come in, ma'am. I will see if she is busy." Pointing to a small room she asked Ellen to wait. The room had not changed in all the years since Ellen had first stood in it. She put a hand to her chest and drew in a long, slow breath, willing herself to calm down and her heart to stop pounding.

Matron approached and to Ellen's dismay she recognized her as the same Mrs. Shaw who had taken her from her mother so many years ago. She looked much older now but there was no mistaking her cold eyes. She reached to shake Ellen's hand.

Barely breathing, Ellen said, "I remember you from long ago. I was one of the girls you sent to Canada."

"Oh, I do not send children to Canada or

anywhere else," the woman answered, drawing herself up. "I only follow orders from my superiors."

Ellen's jaw dropped but she willed herself to recover her composure. She needed information from this odious woman so it would not do to upset Mrs. Shaw or she might not find out what she needed to know.

Mrs. Shaw admitted remembering Ellen's mother. She invited Ellen to her study to have tea and after the two of them had settled into a pair of leather-covered chairs she explained a little of what she knew of Ellen's mother's situation and what had caused her to bring Ellen to the home. "We communicated a long time ago," she said, "but in the past several years I have heard nothing at all. I may have a few addresses of other family members and your mother's old address if you think that would help. Maybe you could follow those up. I'm sorry, but that's all I have."

Ellen took down the information, thanked Mrs. Shaw for her help and left. As the front door closed behind her she took a deep breath. Seeing Mrs. Shaw as a frail, old woman had been a shock to Ellen. In her mind the matron had remained a huge, threatening ogre, still sometimes entering her dreams and scaring her. Now she could no longer find it in her heart to hate or fear the woman. As she walked back down the gravel drive to the big iron gates, she felt a lightness that she had not experienced in years.

When she returned to the city, she searched her handbag for the address Susan had given her and decided to look up Susan's son. She longed to be with someone kind after her visit to Hope House.

It did not take her long to find the street. Stanley and Anna welcomed her into their home once she explained who she was and how she had come to be standing on their doorstep. "Come in, love," Stanley said, opening the door wide. "How was Ma? She's a right little goer, isn't she? Never still for a minute. Fair tires me out, she does, even though she's twice my age," he said with a hint of pride. "You're welcome to use our place as a home base while you search for your family."

Overwhelmed at their generosity and more than a little relieved, she gratefully accepted. Describing her visit to Hope House as Anna showed her to her room, she said, "I must admit I did not want to be alone right now."

## Chapter Thirty-eight

The next day, Stan was up early for work and Anna made sure Ellen had a hearty breakfast before she left the house. Stan had drawn maps for Ellen to find the addresses of her relatives. Anna said, "You come back at any time. I plan to be home all day. I am so curious to hear how your day goes and I hope you find what you are looking for."

Ellen set out to find the first person on the list, her Aunt Rose. The address indicated that she lived in an area called Kingstanding. Ellen caught a tram then had to walk quite a long distance until she found the house. She stood on the street outside and studied it. As big and ugly as ever with paint peeling off the front door, it squatted next to the broken pavement like a worn-out shoe. When she knocked, an explosion of noise erupted from within. In a few minutes, a young girl pulled open the door.

"I'm looking for a lady named Rose," she explained, almost hoping that her aunt did not live there.

The girl turned and yelled over her shoulder. "Hey mum, someone here to see you."

The woman who came to the door was short and fat with lank, greasy hair – almost exactly how Ellen had remembered her. Except for the lines on her haggard face, she had hardly changed a bit.

Rose stared at the lovely young woman standing on her doorstep as recognition flickered across her startled features. "You must be our Mary's girl, Ellen! You look just like her."

Ellen reached out to shake her hand. "Are you my Aunt Rose?"

"Yes, I am" she stammered. She could not believe that Ellen was standing in front of her wearing beautiful clothes, her hair tied back with a green, satin ribbon. "Good Lord, I never expected to see you again in my life." She threw open the door and hollered, "Come in, love."

The inside of the house looked much as Ellen remembered. It was clear that nothing in Rose's life had changed and the smell of yesterday's cabbage still hung in the air. Ellen followed her aunt through to the back of the house, past the room where she had lived with her mother, Sammy and Sarah, and into the grimy living room. She had forgotten the filth but not the violence between her aunt and uncle and now that memory rushed back, too. Her stomach convulsed and she wanted to turn and run back out that door but she could not because she needed to find out about her mother. She swallowed hard and tried not to show how repulsed she felt by everything. She perched on the edge of a grubby chair that her aunt offered her.

Rose bustled about in the kitchen making tea. "How long have you been here?" she asked, wiping a dirty mug on a soiled apron and filling it with muddy, brown tea.

Ellen eyed the tea then set the mug down on the rickety table next to her elbow without taking a drink. "I have so many questions," she told her aunt, "and I am hoping you can help me answer them."

She quickly summarized her life story, recounting how she had been transported to Canada at the age of nine. Ellen relayed only the scantest details.

"Oh, dear, how terrible," Rose gasped. "The family had no idea anything like that had happened."

"What can you tell me about my mother?"

"After she left you at the home, she almost had a nervous breakdown," Rose told her. "She struggled to keep Sam and Sarah with her and never stopped saying she wished she had never given you up. She has never stopped talking about you."

When Ellen heard this, she didn't know what to think. She had spent years resenting her mother and harboring so much anger towards her that it never occurred to her that her mother even cared.

"Your mother managed to find a job in a store not long after she gave you up. She did well there and was finally been able to rent a place on her own." Rose looked sheepishly at Ellen. "I think she was glad to get away from me, if you want to know the truth. I was a right cow towards her," she admitted. "But we are all right now. Friends, as it should be. She met a very nice man named Charles Shipton and they have been married a few years now. Sam and Sarah still live at home."

Rose gave her the address for her mother's house. "It's not far from here. You can walk there."

As she was leaving Ellen slipped some money into her Aunt's hand knowing it would most likely go for drink, but somehow she suddenly felt sorry for her. "Please don't tell my mother I am here just yet. I plan to visit her tomorrow but I have a lot to think about this evening."

"Of course, love. I promise I won't say a word," Rose said, tapping the side of her nose and winking.

"She is going to be over the moon to see you, though. Ta-ra, love," she said, as she closed the door behind Ellen. With money in her hand now she grabbed her purse and slipped on her shoes. Chuckling to herself, she headed for the back lane.

# Chapter Thirty-nine

Ellen decided to go back to Stan's house as she needed a little time to be alone before confronting her mother. She felt like her emotions had been rung out like a wet tea towel and she wanted time to digest everything that she had learned that day.

At Stan's place Ellen told her hosts about her day. She described her Aunt Rose and frowned. "When I was young, living with her was a test of endurance and certainly not for the faint-hearted. The knock-out fighting and cursing would curl your ears back then and as I sat in her living room today, the memories all came back. She seems different now, though; a lot softer. I think I could like her," she said then grimacing, she laughed. "But definitely not that suspect tea."

The next morning Ellen was again up early and anxious to be on her way. As before, Anna insisted on feeding her a huge breakfast. With the address written on a slip of paper that she clutched in her hand she followed Stan's directions and found the right tram.

Finally, Ellen stood on the street where her mother lived and as she walked toward the house, her legs felt weak. *What if she's not home?* she worried. She turned up the walk toward the front door.

The door opened almost immediately when she knocked; almost as though her mother had been waiting for her to arrive. A strangled cry escaped Ellen's lips. Suddenly, she felt seven years old again.

Mary looked at the beautiful young woman standing before her. She gasped and her eyes filled with tears. "Ellen" she cried, reaching for her. In the next moment they were in each others' arms, sobbing as choked words tumbled out.

"Let me look at you," Mary cried, wiping tears from her eyes. "I can hardly believe that you're home at last. You've grown up and you are so beautiful."

"I wasn't sure if you would want to see me again," Ellen murmured.

"I have wanted nothing else since that horrible day when I left you at the home." Mary took Ellen's hand and drew her into the living room. Sitting side by side on the sofa, Mary began to tell Ellen her side of their story beginning with how difficult her life had become after Ellen's father died of the fever.

"I tried to get you back from that home but they would not even let me visit you. I no idea whether you were still in that place or not. They told me it would be better if I didn't see you. That broke my heart but I had no way to get to you."

Ellen had never known this and, sitting there, she felt the hard shell around her heart start to crack and crumble away. Her mother had not abandoned her after all and she had never stopped loving her. Ellen told her mother a little of her hard life in Canada and about the loss of her little son, Robbie.

Mary reached out and gathered Ellen in her arms, "Oh, my dear child," she murmured. "You have suffered so much heartbreak, so much pain."

Ellen had spent years dreaming that her mother would hold her like this and comfort her and now it was really happening.

"Sam and Sarah will be home later," Mary said, stroking Ellen's hair. "They are out at work now, so you must stay until they come home. They will be so thrilled to see you."

Over steaming cups of tea, they settled down to catch up on their lost years. Getting to know each other again after so much time apart, both women had a lot to share. Mary told her about her new husband, Charles, and what a good man he was. "Your father was wonderful man and a devoted father," she said. "He loved you very much." She filled in the missing details of Ellen's past. For both of them, it was like gathering up the lost pieces of a jigsaw puzzle and finally being able to put it all together.

"Your grandmother is still alive and living not too far away," Mary said. "She will be thrilled to see you again."

After several hours, Ellen finally felt that she understood why her mother had been forced to give her up. A great, heavy load lifted from Ellen's heart and at last she was free of the bitterness that she had carried for so many years.

The slanting rays of the setting sun had begun to cast long shadows across the furniture when Mary's husband, Charles, returned home. He walked into the room, looked at the lovely young woman who stood up to greet him and knew instantly that she was the long-lost daughter whose absence his wife had always mourned. It was startling how much she looked like her mother. Mary's eyes shone with joy and as Charles took Ellen's hand, he said, "I'm so happy to meet you at last. You have made your mother a very happy woman today."

A few minutes later the door opened and in walked a tall, young man who matched Ellen's faded memories of her father. Ellen stood up to introduce herself but before she could say a word he rushed to her and threw his arms around her, swinging her off her feet. "Ellen, you've come home," Sam cried. "How I have missed you all these years! I have always wondered what happened to you."

"Oh, Sam," Ellen said. "Just look at you. You're all grown up."

A few minutes later Sarah arrived. Though she was excited to meet her sister, she had been so young when Ellen left that she did not remember her.

"You were just a baby when I last saw you," Ellen said, "and now you've grown up and become so beautiful." She stroked Sarah's long, straight blonde hair.

With her whole family around her, Ellen felt a sense of belonging that she had ached for all her life and she felt like now her wounded heart could begin to heal. Finally, as it neared twilight, Ellen said it was time for her to return to Stan's and Anna's home. Her mother's house had no room and she knew that Stan and Anna would be anxious to hear her news.

Back at their house, Ellen told Stan and Anna about everything that had happened that day. The couple was genuinely thrilled for her and the three of them talked well into the early hours of the next morning. Finally Ellen said, "I'm exhausted and need to go to bed." She picked up her sweater and trudged up the stairs. Closing the door to her room, she changed into her nightgown and tumbled into bed. Then pulling the covers up under her chin, she drifted off to sleep in a reverie of happiness. She had come full circle and had finally found her way home again.

# Chapter Forty

As the days went by, Ellen and Mary strengthened the bond that had been so cruelly torn apart those many years ago. These were such happy days and Ellen prayed that they would never end.

Mary took Ellen to meet her grandmother who had such played a big part in Ellen's early years. By now, Clare had grown old and frail but she was so ecstatic to see her granddaughter that tears sprang into her old, rheumy eyes and she could not stop smiling and touching Ellen. She had loved this little girl so much and missed her so terribly. Now that the lost child had come home again, she finally felt that she could die at peace.

Mary told Ellen that her grandparents on her father's side had long since passed away. Tommy's bitter mother had remained in a sanatorium and had never found it in her cold heart to forgive her only son for marrying Mary.

"Do you remember your granddad, Ellen?" Mary asked.

Ellen thought for a moment before the image of his face swam into her memory. "Yes," she said, in wonder, "I do remember him. Why did he stop coming to see us?"

"Bless his soul," Mary answered, "he died of a heart attack shortly before I put you in the home. He did his best to help me but his health declined and there was only so much he could do after your father died and Gladys went into the sanatorium. I think the loss of his only son just broke him."

"Oh, Mum." Ellen said. "You did what you had to do. Don't blame yourself."

"No," Mary replied. "There's no point crying over what might have been." Changing the subject, she asked, "Do you plan to stay in Birmingham? Maybe you could find work in your trade as a florist."

"I really don't know yet," Ellen said. "There is so much for me to take in after all this time. I'm not sure what to do or where I should live. I want to be near you, Mom." She reached for Mary's hand and squeezed her fingers. "It's so wonderful to be home again but I shall soon need to find work. I can't sit around drinking tea all day."

Over the weeks that followed Ellen's relationship

with her brother Sam grew and deepened. They had been close as small children and now they had a lot of catching up to do. He showed a keen interest in hearing about her life in Canada. "What was it like?" he asked repeatedly. "I would love to go there." He went to the library and hauled home armloads of books, devouring everything he could find on the country. Each one fired his imagination even more.

Ellen found it hard to encourage him to go to Canada; most of her memories held such sadness and despair. For Ellen, the only bright spot in her time there had been her love for Robbie and her deep friendship with Katie. Many nights she still cried herself to sleep thinking about them. "I was so young when I first went there," she told Sammy, "and I did not have opportunity to go sight-seeing or to enjoy myself. At the home, I was a virtual prisoner then when I lived on the Matthews' farm I lived the life of a slave. Miss Beatrice was kind to me, at first, but then she turned me out on the street when she found out I was to have a child out of wedlock. My life in Canada was seldom happy, so my memories are not pleasant." Based on her own emotions, she tried to dissuade him from considering travelling to Canada, and hope that his interest would wane. Mary also hoped that he would grow bored with his books about the country and stop going on about leaving home and travelling half a world away. She had already lost one child that way. She was terrified of losing her only son, too.

Within a couple of days of starting to look for work, a man named Mr. Newman who owned four flower shops hired Ellen. He desperately needed someone to manage one of them and when Ellen applied he promptly hired her. He had seemed so abrupt and officious during her interview that she hoped she would not have to see too much of him.

Ellen soon settled into her new job and she found a furnished flat to rent near the shop she managed. Situated on the main floor of a beautiful Victorian house, it had a large living room painted a lovely delicate green with white trim and soft cream muslin curtains that draped to the floor. Around an ornate fireplace, two comfortable chairs and a small settee in a floral pattern of autumn colors had been arranged to enjoy the heat from the grate. The suite also featured a dining room with white paneling, and a crystal chandelier hanging over a table with six carved chairs. A small modern kitchen looked out on a back garden as did the bedroom which had been painted lilac. Ellen found it pleasing and comfortable.

# Chapter Forty-one

Winter melted into spring and although her life in England had turned out to be more than she had dreamed, something was missing. She often thought of the small grave back in Canada and sometimes woke in the night thinking she had heard her son calling.

One day Mary asked her, "Is something wrong? You seem so troubled lately."

"Oh Mom, I really don't know. I should be so content now that I have found my family. I have a job I that like and a lovely little home. Why do I feel as though a big part of me is missing? I can't understand why I feel so unsettled."

Mary listened in sympathy then holding her hand, she looked into her daughter's eyes. "Can I tell you what I think?" Ellen nodded. "My darling, you have not finished grieving for your little boy, Robbie. A part of you has never left that country. I experienced the same kind of pain all those years we were apart," Mary said. "Maybe you should think about taking a trip back to Canada. You are not yet sure where you belong. I think you need to know in your heart that the Canadian part of your life is behind you. That may be the only way you will find certainty. If you do decide to go, my prayer will be that you find some peace. Of course, I hope your decision will be to return to England to be near us, but if Canada is your choice we will all adjust. I want you to be happy, whatever you decide."

That night when Ellen returned to her home she knew that her mother had given her a lot to think about. She had not considered ever going back to Canada but she felt torn, being in England and knowing that Robbie lay across the ocean. This must be why she felt so sad all the time, she reasoned. When she had first met her family, she felt sure that being with them would be the answer but after a time the sadness had returned and she went through her days carrying the memory of her son in her heart.

After a restless night she woke with a new determination. She must go back to the country where she had known so much unhappiness. At the same time, she knew that part of her heart still remained there with Robbie and Katie.

A few days later, while working on a flower arrangement for a wedding, the bell over the shop's front door chimed and Mr. Newman strode in. Ellen set down her clippers.

"Ellen," he began, "I've been meaning to speak with you for some time."

"Is something wrong?"

"Oh, no, no. Nothing like that." He cleared his throat and pushed a fallen petal with his toe. "No," he said again. "It's just that I was wondering if you would like to go boating with me tomorrow on the pond in the park. The weather is fine and we could take a picnic. Will you come?"

She picked up her clippers, snipped a stem then put them down again. "Yes," she answered, nonplussed. "That would very nice."

# Chapter Forty-two

Ellen visited her mother to discuss her plans to travel back to Canada. When Sam came home, he listened intently then asked, "Can I go with you? We would be good company for each other. Canada sounds so exciting to me after all you have told me about it." He could not hide his eagerness to go.

Mary felt grieved to think that once again she must say goodbye to her lovely daughter, and now her only son wanted to go away, too. Though she fully understood Ellen's need, it did not ease the pain of seeing them preparing to go.

After much planning and arranging, passage was finally booked to Canada six weeks hence, which would give Ellen's employer time to find a replacement for her position. Since their day boating in the park he had taken her to dinner twice and they had gone once to the theatre. Though he frequently asked her to spend more time with him,

Ellen had been reluctant to encourage a relationship with him.

Once her ticket had been booked, Ellen called Mr. Newman and asked him to come to the store at the end of the working day.

"I asked you here to let you know I am going away for a while, Mr. Newman," Ellen told him when he arrived. "I am not sure for how long I will be gone but will be leaving in about six weeks. I wanted to give you lots of notice so you have time to find someone to replace me."

"Going away?" he sputtered. "Where are you going?"

"I plan to return to Canada," she answered. "I find that I have unfinished business that I must attend to. I'm sorry to give you such short notice but it was quite a sudden decision. My brother will be travelling with me."

"I had no idea you were not happy here," he said, running his fingers through his dark hair. "Is there anything I can do to change your mind?" He reached for Ellen's hand.

Ellen slipped her hand away and stepped back. "No," she replied. "My passage has already been booked and paid for and I have no reason to change my plans." The other staff had gone home for the day and Ellen was alone in the shop now with her boss. He walked over to the door and locked it. Ellen sensed that he had something to say but could not imagine what it might be. Finally, he turned to her. "As you know, Ellen, I am a widower. My wife passed away almost two years ago after a long illness with cancer."

"Yes," Ellen told him, "you have told me that."

"I think we have had some wonderful times together, you and me," he continued. "When my wife died I thought I would like to die, too. I could not think of any reason to go on living."

"I understand that, Mr. Newman," Ellen said. "I lost my little son and my best friend in a terrible accident. That is one of the reasons that I have to go back to Canada."

"Yes, yes," he said, pacing back and forth across the shop floor. "What I want you to know is that my life began to look up the day you walked through that door asking for a job."

"Oh," said Ellen, stepping backwards again. "I had no idea."

"Ellen, in our work together I have come to care for you a great deal. You've probably noticed that I have begun to spend more and more time at this shop than at any of the others, haven't you?"

Ellen had noticed but thought that he had been checking her work even though she suspected there was more to it. Since she had been pre-occupied with preparing for her trip, she had not given his added attentions much thought. Now she could see that indeed, he had been spending a great deal of time at her shop and seemed to want to spend more time with her. The pieces of this puzzle began to fall into place.

"I thought I would have plenty of time to tell you this but with you planning to go away, I can't afford to wait. I have fallen in love with you." He turned to her and looked into her eyes. "I don't want you to leave now. Will you stay?"

"I don't know what to say, Mr. Newman," Ellen began, her emotions reeling. "I had no idea that you felt this way. You didn't say."

"Oh, Ellen," he replied, reaching for her hands again. This time she allowed him to take hers in his own. "Please don't leave. I have already lost one woman I loved. I can't bear to lose another."

"Mr. Newman, this is all very sudden for me. I'm immensely flattered by your feelings toward me but my plans to go to Canada have already been made. This is something I must do."

His face fell and he looked so downcast that Ellen felt tempted to change her mind and stay, but she remained silent.

"Promise me, then," he said, "that you will

remember me and when you come back you will consider my offer."

"What offer is that, Mr. Newman? Are you promising me my job back?"

He laughed lightly. "Of course," he said, "you may have your job back. But I am asking you if you would consider becoming my wife. I could not let you leave without telling you how I feel. Please take as much time as you need to think about this. Just tell me if you think there is a chance that you could love me."

"Yes, there is a chance," she replied, "but first I need to make this journey, and I can't make any promises until I have. Please understand."

"All right," he said. "I will wait. But do you think you could call me William instead of Mr. Newman? I believe we have an understanding then, don't we?"

"Yes," she replied. "You could say that."

"In that case, may I kiss you?"

Ellen's heart leapt in her breast as the memory of Vincent's passionate, treacherous kisses raced across her mind. *This man is not Vincent*, she told herself firmly. *In fact, he is nothing like him at all.* She took a deep breath.

"I think that would be fine," she said in a small voice.

William took her in his arms and tenderly kissed her. Her head swam and her knees grew weak. She didn't want to have these feelings but she found that couldn't help it.

"I will be waiting for you when you return," he said when he finally pulled away from her. "I hope it will not take too long for you to do what you have to do. When you return we can make plans," he said, kissing her once more. But Ellen didn't know if she would ever return. She would not know until she had been to Canada and faced her ghosts.

That evening, Ellen told Mary what had happened between her and her boss, Mr. Newman. "My plans have not changed," she said. "I still need to go and say a final farewell to Robbie and Katie. I hope I am able to close that chapter of my life once and for all."

# Chapter Forty-three

A few weeks later Sam and Ellen stood on the deck of a ship and waved good-bye to William and to her mother and Sarah. As the ship sailed away from the docks she remembered the voyage she had taken as a little girl and recalled how she had searched the crowd, hoping against hope to see her mother. This time, though, her mother stood on the dock and waved her handkerchief in good-bye.

It seemed that in no time at all they arrived at the docks in Halifax. The last time she had arrived, the wealthy people in their furs had been the first to disembark and the poor children from below decks had watched, shivering in the cold, knowing that their own futures were filled with uncertainty.

Holding her brother's arm, she smiled. "Come on, Sam. Let's go. We must find a hotel and get settled then make a plan of action." They travelled by taxi to a small hotel that the driver recommended. The hotel was old but well maintained. Walking into a cheerful, spacious lobby they found bright, overstuffed chairs scattered about and a few guests relaxing, smoking and reading newspapers.

After checking in, they were shown to a suite on the second floor with two bedrooms. She tipped the boy who placed her luggage on a stand near the door.

"We certainly did not have beds like these the first time I arrived in this country," she told Sam as she bounced on one. Walking to the window, she pushed the heavy velvet curtains back and looked out at the busy street below. "Oh yes," she said. "This time is very different."

The next morning after breakfast in the hotel's pleasant dining room, they were ready to start the day. Ellen told Sam she planned to visit Hope House again.

"What will you do today?" she asked, since he had already told her he did not want to accompany her there.

"I want to explore," he said. "There is so much to see and from the glimpse I had yesterday, I can't wait." They agreed to meet for dinner back at the hotel.

After making enquiries at the front desk Ellen caught a tram and was soon standing at the door of Hope House. A cheery, robust woman answered, mopping her face with an apron as she blew a few wisps of hair away from her face.

"Yes, my dear, what can I do for you?"

Ellen asked if she could see Matron.

Opening the door wider, the lady said, "Come on in. I'll see if she's busy."

Leading Ellen to a small office, she commented, "It is certainly a hot day. I am making buns but I think it's too hot for baking. Well, you wait here and I'll try to find Matron for you."

Ellen sat down and looked around with interest. She had never been in this part of the house. The atmosphere of the place seemed much more relaxed than when she had stayed there. A cluttered desk sat at the far end of the room and lots of bookshelves lined the walls. Large windows let in the light and dust motes floated in the sun's rays. Ellen's hand stroked the arm of the dark leather chair. An identical one stood opposite her with a small glass table in between. Interestingly, the room had a masculine feel so she was a little surprised when an elderly woman bustled in with an enquiring look in her eyes. The woman who had answered the door followed her in.

Ellen stood up to shake her hand. "Hello," she said. "Thank you for seeing me. My name is Ellen Clarke."

"Please be seated. My name is Mrs. Bower. How may I help you?"

"Well, it is quite a long story really. I am hoping you could answer a few questions for me."

Leaning forward, she tapped Ellen's knee. "Well, in that case, we should have a nice cup of coffee, wouldn't you say?" Without waiting for an answer, she turned to her companion. "Eleanor, would you have time to make us some coffee, and maybe bring us some of your sweet buns. Your baking is wonderful and the buns are so delicious, fresh from the oven."

"I think I can manage that," Eleanor said, glowing with pleasure at the compliment as she left the room.

Mrs. Bower smiled at Ellen. "That works every time," she said, laughing and winking conspiratorially. "Now tell me what you need to know."

Ellen told her the story of how she had been one of many children transported to Canada from England. She described the deplorable treatment she had received after being sent to the Mathews' farm and the abuse at the hands of Ed Mathews. "I am curious to know if children are still being sent to that farm, Mrs. Bower. If they are, they're not safe. He is a horrible and dangerous man. All these years it has worried me to think of other young girls forced to be at his mercy."

"I have only recently been assigned to this home but I assure you I will look into this situation and make it high priority. I will pull the file on this family and, if there is a child there, I will make sure he or she is removed immediately. I am so sorry you went through that ordeal at such a tender age, my dear," she said. "It should never have happened. I promise you that with any children under my care from now on, prospective homes will be carefully monitored."

"I appreciate that, Mrs. Bower," Ellen said.

"Thank-you for coming here to tell me this. You have done a great service to the children. I wish there was not a need for a charity such as Hope House but sadly, there is. If it is managed well, it can be a positive experience for the children and that's how it should be, even though taking them away from their parents can be traumatic. Perhaps you would consider becoming involved with the children's care here. We are always looking for more help."

Ellen shook her head. "That's not possible for me now."

After plenty of coffee and delicious buns, Ellen left the home feeling exhilarated and elated. Mrs. Bower's willingness to hear her story and her compassion for Ellen's suffering felt like a healing balm for her injured soul.

Sam had also just returned to the hotel when Ellen arrived. Filled with news about his day, he was fairly bursting to share his adventures with Ellen. He had visited museums, shops and theatres and loved them all. Over dinner they talked about their day. It seemed that both had found satisfaction in the day's activities and both looked forward to what the next day would hold.

# Chapter Forty-four

The next morning, Ellen told Sam, "I intend to visit Robbie's and Katie's graves but it will take two days on the train to get to Toronto. I understand if you do not want to come with me."

"Oh, I want to come," he said. "He was my nephew and I think we should go together. Besides, I don't want to miss the chance to see more of the country."

Two days later, they reached the place where Ellen had known the happiest and saddest times of her life. They found a hotel close to the train station and the next day they caught a tram to the church near where she had lived. Ellen pointed out familiar streets as they passed by but her heart felt heavy with sadness. She remembered little Robbie as he had toddled along these very sidewalks, interested in everything around him. Katie had laughed and scolded him at the same time. It seemed such a long time ago.

Sam noticed the change in Ellen but said nothing. Reaching for her hand, he squeezed it. Ellen turned towards him, her eyes bright with unshed tears, and her lips trembled as she tried to smile. The tram conductor called out their stop and, jumping down, they started walking to the churchyard. It was a lovely, warm day and flowers bloomed in boxes along the street. A gentle breeze blew, cooling them, and as they passed a flower-seller on the sidewalk, they stopped and purchased pretty bunches of mixed flowers to place on the graves. At the end of the block they turned the corner and could see the lovely, old church up on a hill.

Making her way through the churchyard, Ellen walked straight to the resting places of Robbie and Katie. Sam placed his flowers on the graves, studied the gravestones for a moment, then walked away to allow Ellen to be alone.

Ellen gently arranged the flowers on Robbie's grave first. Sitting beside the tiny grave, she sobbed. "Oh, my darling Robbie, I had to come. I miss you so much. I try to find comfort knowing you have your Aunty Katie with you but I wish you were here with me still." Putting her lips to the gravestone, she whispered, "Sleep well, my angel, until we meet again."

Moving to Katie's grave, she could almost feel her dear friend standing beside her. "Katie, I miss you so much. I have found my family in England and things are well. I met a wonderful man called William who says he loves me. Perhaps one day we will be married. I think you would like him."

Ellen closed her eyes. Just then she felt sure a hand slipped into hers. She did not move yet somehow she knew it was Katie's. Then a soft voice whispered in her ear, "Robbie is happy and I am taking good care of him. We shall all be together again one day, but not yet. You have important things to do so leave us now and be happy." Then like a soft sigh, it was over.

Ellen opened her eyes and looked around. Katie's presence had seemed so real but knew she would not see her. Still, somehow the pain in her heart had eased a little. She stood up and brushed the grass from her skirt. Walking towards where Sammy leaned against a headstone she felt more light-hearted than she had for years.

Sammy turned to look at her. She seemed different to him now. The look of anguish that had been there before had gone. She actually looked happy. He reached out, put an arm around her shoulder and pulled her close. Sam knew she had found what she had been searching for. After a

while, he took Ellen's hand and they slowly walked
away from the graveyard.

# Chapter Forty-five

"What are your plans now, Ellen?" Sam asked her over lunch at their hotel.

"There is someone in England named William, who has made me an interesting offer but first I think you and I should spend some time together here before we go back. You've seen almost nothing of this huge country. We could take a few trips and do some exploring. Would you like that?"

"I would love that," Sammy replied, "but I should warn you that I have decided not return to England with you. I plan to stay for a while and travel to the different provinces. I have spoken with a few people who say that there are endless miles of prairie land in the west then mountains higher than anything I've ever seen before. I must see it. I have loved what little I have seen so far. I think I can find work as I go and I want to try. I hope you will understand and explain to mom how I feel."

Ellen searched his face. She could see the desire for adventure shining in his eyes. "Oh Sam, are you sure? It's a big decision. Where will you stay? What kind of work will you do?"

He laughed. "Don't worry about me. Finding out is half the fun of it. Now, let's just enjoy the time we have together before you leave. Show me this city, all the places you can remember."

That evening they went out for dinner. "You know Ellen," Sam said, "I have not told you this before but I want you to know how proud I am of you. You have managed to overcome so many things in your life. I think your experiences have made you the strong, independent woman you are today and whatever you choose to do from now on, you will do it well."

Never in Ellen's life had anyone told her that she was someone to admire and of whom they could be proud.

"Oh, Sam," she said, tears stinging her eyes, "I think that's the kindest thing anyone has ever said to me."

Three weeks later, Ellen stood once more on the deck of a ship that would take her home to England. Exhausted from nonstop sightseeing and Sam's irrepressible enthusiasm, she had hugged her brother good-bye on the dock.

"Don't worry," she promised, "I will explain everything to our mom.

Make sure you come home soon, though. We shall miss you."

Now, after waving to her brother until he was nothing more than a speck in the distance, she walked away from the rail. She thought of her mother and sister awaiting her return and of the man who had professed his love for her.

"To be going home is a wonderful feeling," she said to herself. "It's a wonderful feeling, indeed."

## THE END

# Afterword

Ellen was my mother. She was one of thousands of British children transported to Canada, and other countries, as a solution to the severe poverty in England in the late 1800s and early 1900s.

Parents unable to feed their children were encouraged to use charity homes temporarily in the hope that they could recover them once the family's fortunes improved. When they sought this solution, most did not realize that their children could end up being transported to foreign lands.

Though this story is based on my mother's life, I have fictionalized it and concluded it in the way I would have like my mother's life to have ended.

My mother spoke little about her childhood experiences of being transported to Canada but in communications with the charity homes in England and Canada, I was able to fill in a lot of gaps about my mother's young life.

Many children who experienced this trauma have, even as adults, been reluctant to talk about their lives. Often the pain of remembering is still too great, since many never saw their families again.

My mother, Ellen, worked as a servant with a family and her experience was similar to that of

Ellen in the story. Though the names have been changed, families like the Mathews' were all too common and children were frequently abused, raped, or neglected.

When my mother returned to England after a long struggle to save enough money for her passage, the reunion with her family did not go well. Though her mother welcomed her back, Ellen could never cope with all the rage and disappointment she carried from being sent away. Knowing that her brother and sister had not been put in the home, she could never manage to deal with her own feelings of rejection. It was not long until she turned her back on her family and cut off all ties with her mother.

My father, William, (Mr. Newman in the story) was a kind, gentle man. He worked in a factory in England.

Growing up with my mother was difficult. She had four children; three girls and one boy, Jean, Graham, Yvonne, and me, Diane. Because of her lack of normal parenting, she had no emotional coping skills and consequently was often self-indulgent and unfeeling. Any disagreement or confrontation amongst us would cause her to completely close down emotionally and she seemed most comfortable when the home was filled with conflict and tension.

We were an emotionally volatile family. My eldest sister, Jean, had the worst time. Home life for her was difficult since our mother treated her little better than she herself had been treated as a child. Jean was forced to act as a caregiver to her younger siblings and expected to do most of the housework from a very young age.

It took me years to grasp the reasons for my mother's peculiar behavior but now I understand that she was doing the best she could.

In my research, I discovered that when my grandmother (Mary) found out that her daughter had been sent to another country, she tried very hard to have her returned to England. I was able to obtain many of the letters that she had written over the years to the charity home in Canada. My mother never knew about her own mother's letters. How I wish my mother had known of them for then she may not have been so bitter towards her family. But who knows? Those were different and difficult times and we will never how things might have been. I am thankful that the practice of giving up one's children to charity homes no longer goes on in our country today.

In 1967, I immigrated to Canada with my husband, Barry. When I told my mother I was going to Canada she was horrified. She had spoken very little of her life in Canada, so naturally I did not understand her reaction. On the rare occasions that I managed to get her to talk to me about some of her experiences, she revealed little. I wish now that I had encouraged her to tell me much more. I also wish she had been able to know the Canada that I know. I feel sure she would have changed her opinion had she seen the country through different eyes.

Sadly, before she had the chance to visit, she died of cancer in 1972. During this trying time of her illness, she reconciled with her own younger sister. At that time I was able to meet my aunt who I found to be a very nice lady. I fervently hope that renewing the relationship with her own sister gave my mother some peace in her dying days.

Writing this story, although it is only loosely based on my mother's story, has helped me to understand her more than I ever could have otherwise and for that I am so grateful.

*Diane Wild*
Contact the author by email at <u>diane.wild@gmail.com</u>.

Also by Diane Wild:

At the age of ninety-four, Louise is left with only her memories and plenty of time to reflect on her life. As a child, Louise knew that her mother did her best to protect the children from her father's violent rages. When her drunken father suddenly dies, the penniless family is cast into the streets. Taking with them only what they can carry, Louise and her mother, Clare, and her young brother, Freddy, take to the roads, seeking help and work wherever Clare might find it. Fate intervenes when Clare finds a job at the Old Manor, home to Dr. John Bower, a prominent country physician. Louise believes that life will be pleasant and secure from then on. It is, until Dr. Bower's reprehensible cousin, Thomas, arrives, changing Louise's world forever.

www.ingramcontent.com/pod-product-compliance
Lightning Source LLC
Chambersburg PA
CBHW032032240626
47154CB00003B/876